RUN TO ME

THE CLARKE BROTHERS: BOOK THREE

LILIAN MONROE

Cover photo by Regina Wamba
Cover design by PopKitty Designs

ISBN 13: 978-1-922457-22-6

1

————

ZOE

"Good luck tomorrow, monkey." My heart squeezes. My hand tightens around my cell phone, even though I know that there's no way I can make it to my daughter's piano recital. It still makes me feel like a bad mother to miss it.

"I'm not a monkey, Mom," Audrey answers with a sigh. "And I'm not small. Could a monkey play piano?"

"Not as well as you," I smile. "Alright come on, put your grandmother back on the phone."

"Grandma!" Audrey yells straight into the receiver. I pull the phone away from my ear and cringe as she yells. I listen as their phone exchanges hands and smile when I hear Audrey humming in the background.

"You'll record her recital for me?" I ask when my mother comes on the phone. My voice is trembling, and I swallow to keep it steady.

"Every minute of it, Zoe. Don't worry."

"I'm not worried. Just... disappointed. This will be the longest I've been away from her since she was born."

"Don't torture yourself," my mother says. I can almost see her pursing her lips and shaking her head. "You daughter will be fine. She'll be great, actually. You'll realize she doesn't need you at all, and it'll make you feel happy and heartbroken at the same time. Take it from someone who knows," she adds ruefully. "Just finish this job and come back. This contract will be sorted out in no time, and everything will be back to normal."

As much as I want to fight it, my mother's platitudes help. Her words are comforting and my shoulders start to relax. I nod.

As if she can see me nod from the other end of the phone, my mom speaks again. This time her voice is soft, and it sounds like a warm hug.

"And Zoe?" she asks, letting my name hang in the air.

I clear my throat. "Yeah, Mom?"

"Try and enjoy yourself. You're a beautiful, successful single woman. You have some time for yourself now, for the first time since Mark passed. Make the most of it. We'll be fine. Won't we, Audrey?" she adds, slightly louder. I hear Audrey giggle in the background.

"Of course!" comes my daughter's voice in the distance

I smile. "Give her a big hug for me, okay?"

"I will. Now go. Go to the town bar, have a drink, and relax. I'm your mother and I still get to tell you what to do once in a while."

I chuckle and take a deep breath. "Sounds like something I can manage."

"Good. I love you, Zoe. This will all be over soon. Don't worry about a thing."

My throat tightens and I nod my head. When I speak, my voice is barely a whisper. "I love you too, Mom. Thank you."

"Don't mention it. Now go and get yourself a drink!"

I laugh and we hang up the call. I'm sitting on the edge of my hard hotel bed without moving. I stare at my phone's blank screen and take a deep breath.

She's right. It's only a couple months, and I already know that Audrey will be fine. If anything, it's me who will suffer from the separation the most. She's busy with school and soccer and piano, with her friends and with her grandmother. She'll hardly think about me at all.

Now me, on the other hand... That's a different story. When Audrey's father, my husband, died of cancer when she was two, I felt like my heart would never recover. I still don't know if it has, and it's been just over six years. It's been alright to be alone, because I've had her. Now she's on the other side of the country and I'm kind of freaking out.

For the hundredth time since I got to my hotel, I look at the dingy room and sigh. I try not to breathe too deeply, because the air in the room is stuffy and smells vaguely of mildew. I get up as the bedsprings squeak, avoiding my reflection in the mirror hanging on the wall. I don't want to be reminded of how old and tired I surely look. Being a single mother with an active job will do that to a person.

I run my fingers over the file on the desk: my assignment. Or rather, my punishment, as I've come to see it. I knew that working for a bureaucratic entity like the government could be difficult, but I never imagined I'd get relegated to the middle of nowhere for trying to show initiative. Now I have to implement my forest fire management systems in a National Park on the opposite side of the country.

I should probably be flattered. It's supposed to be an honor to be sent here, since governments are usually so slow to implement new programs. But the fire that happened here in Lang Creek last year shook the entire Parks community, and my boss volunteered me up as a tribute. Or 'gave me the opportunity of a lifetime,' as he described it.

I sigh, shaking my head. Maybe my mom is right. I just need to relax. Tomorrow I drive down to the shitty little town that I've been assigned to, and I'll deal with it then. For now I just need to empty my mind and relax. If I go to the bar and grab a drink, maybe the aching loneliness inside me will go away just a little, and I won't be worried about what my daughter is doing every minute that I'm away from her.

I swear I've never been a helicopter mom, but being a couple thousand miles away from your only child will do that to a person.

I slip out the door and get in the elevator. I glance in the lobby bar and keep walking. It's dark and empty in there, with dated decor and a slight sense of melancholy. Not what I need right now.

I'm not sure what I do need, but I head down the road toward the strip of shops and bars that I saw on the drive in. Calling it 'downtown' is a bit generous. Soon, I can hear music and people as I round the corner. I turn into the first bar I see.

It's loud, and dark, and full of people. It's exactly what I wanted. I slip through the crowd and find an empty stool at the end of the bar. It only takes a few moments before the bartender takes my order.

"Gin and soda, please," I say, and he nods. I let my eyes drift across the room and feel my lips curl upwards. Somehow, even now that I'm a grown woman, my mother still knows exactly what I need. I need noise and people and laughter and distractions, so that all the thoughts in my head will be drowned out.

The bartender drops my drink in front of me and I take my first sip with my eyes closed. As soon as the liquid hits my tongue, my eyes fly open and I put the drink down. He must have emptied half the bottle in this glass. The gin tastes fruity and fresh with that indescribable tangy aftertaste. The bartender chuckles as I stare at my glass.

"Looked like you needed it," he grins. "First one's on me."

He's an older man with a huge salt-and-pepper beard. His eyes are dark, but kind. I nod.

"Thanks."

He grins and turns to another customer.

Maybe I do need it. I'm starting to regret not looking at myself in the mirror before leaving. If he can tell I'm stressed, I must look like a mess. I comb my fingers through my hair and wipe my fingers under my eyes, checking them for streaks of mascara. Seeing my fingers come back clean, I take a deep breath and take another sip.

My heartbeat slows down and my eyes relax. I lean my forearms on the bar and let my eyes drift across the room. Something is happening in the corner, like there's a hum of excitement surrounding something.

I turn and see a band starting to set up on a tiny stage. It's more like a step, with barely enough room for the two men to work alongside each other. I lean against the bar, sipping my drink and watching them set up. There are two men setting up the drums and microphones, taking guitars out and testing the sound. The bartender appears beside me and I nod to the band.

"Who are they?"

"Them?" he asks, nodding to the band. "They're the Mad Hatters," he replies. "Play here every second Saturday of the month. Bring the house down every time."

I grunt in acknowledgement and turn back to the band. 'Bringing the house down' must have a different meaning here than in the big city. There's someone new on the step, or the stage, or whatever you'd call it. He's got his back to me, but something in the way he moves makes my heart jump. He's standing tall, and his black t-shirt is stretched across his broad back. I can see the outline of his muscles through the thin fabric. He leans over to pull a cable toward the front, and his shirt lifts up to show the waistband of his underwear.

A blush stains my cheeks.

Why am I blushing? My eyes widen as he turns toward the front, tapping on the microphone and smiling. My heart jumps as I hear his voice over the speakers. It's smooth and deep, and his smile makes a couple girls in the crowd yelp.

"How's everyone doing tonight?"

It's lame and stereotypical. It's what every rock star and wannabe rock star would say, but it still makes the heat rush toward my thighs. He smiles again and slings his guitar over his shoulder, grabbing it and sliding his fingers over the strings. He strums it once and a few more people yell out.

Then, they play. They play and sing and shout and just as the barman said, they bring the house down. I sip my drink and watch as he sings the first song. I don't hear a word. I don't see anything except him, I don't hear anything except the sound of his voice.

2

ETHAN

I ALMOST STOP SINGING and mess up the whole song when she comes out on the dance floor. I catch myself in time, but it's a struggle to keep up. She's dancing like no one is watching, even though everybody in the room is staring at her. She's laughing, and finally, *finally,* she turns toward me.

When she looks at me, it takes all my self-control to keep playing. I'm glad we've rehearsed this song for hours, because at this point, playing the guitar is pure muscle memory. She stares at me and my blood turns to fire. Her lips curl upwards and I can feel myself getting hard.

By the time the first set is done, I have to know who she is. But by the time I put my guitar down she's already disappeared. My eyes scan the crowd and I frown.

Bethany Davis comes up to me, just like she does at every show, and flaps her eyelashes at me.

"Great set, Ethan," she says. She puts her hands on my forearm and presses her chest against me. "Your voice sounds better every week."

"Thanks, Beth," I reply. I take a step back and look over her shoulder. Beth presses her tits against me a bit more and says something that I don't hear. My breath catches in my throat.

There she is.

She's at the bar, in the corner. She's actually sitting in *my* seat. Didn't Carl tell her? He knows that I always sit there, and usually he saves the seat for me.

Not this time. This time, he's let this gorgeous brunette sit on my stool, and he's pouring her another drink. By the time I make it through the crowd to her, she's taking a sip. I watch her lips touch the edge of the glass and my cock pulses.

I clear my throat and tear my eyes away from her, turning to Carl.

"What's this? You're giving away my seat now?" I ask with a grin, glancing back at the woman before turning to Carl.

Carl chuckles. "Didn't think you'd mind," he replies, putting a beer down in front of me. I turn to the woman and let my eyes run up and down her body. I can hardly see straight. She's staring at me with a raised eyebrow and a smile playing in her eyes.

"This is your seat?" she asks. "Didn't see your name on it."

"It's sort of an unwritten rule," I answer, sliding onto the stool next to hers.

She snorts and takes another sip. "You want me to move?" she asks, flashing a mischievous grin at me. My cock is pulsing between my legs and I smile back.

"Nah, you can stay," I answer. *I wouldn't want you to move for anything.* "So you're new in town?"

"Clearly," she answers. "Don't know all the rules yet."

"You'll learn."

She smiles again and shakes her head. "What if I don't like following rules?"

"That would be surprising."

"What, I look nice and innocent to you?"

"Something like that," I reply. "Maybe not innocent," I add. Another smile flashes across her face.

"No," she says slowly, running her finger around the edge of her glass. "Maybe not innocent."

I can't think straight. I know I have to play another set in a few minutes, but right now all I can think of is this woman and how badly I want to fuck her. She tucks a strand of hair behind her ear and I stare at the soft curve of her neck. My eyes drop down to her tits and back up to her face.

God, she's hot.

I clear my throat and shift in my seat, trying to think of something to say. My head is full of cotton and my cock is as hard as steel.

"You're a good dancer," I finally manage to say.

She laughs. "Thanks. You're a good singer."

I turn to her, not sure if she's joking or not. She smiles at me, and I know she isn't. She tilts her head and takes another sip of her drink. I do the same, putting my beer down at the same time as her.

"I'm Zoe," she says, reaching her hand over toward me.

"Ethan," I nod.

I take her hand in mine and ignore the pulsing between my legs. Her skin is soft and warm, and her hand feels like it fits perfectly in my palm. She grabs my hand firmly and shakes it once. Her eyes gleam. A smile stretches her lips as she finally pulls her hand away.

"Are you from here?" she asks, glancing around the bar.

I shake my head. "Nah, I'm from a town a couple hours away," I reply, not taking my eyes off her. "I just come up here to play."

She nods. "I was driving down from the airport and had to take a detour because of the rockslide on the freeway. So I guess you could say I was lucky, otherwise I never would have stopped here."

"You could say that," I reply with a grin. *You could say that I was the lucky one.* I clear my throat, looking away from her to keep my head from spinning. "I drove up to the rock slide this morning," I say, peeling the label off my beer. "It'll take them days to clear the road."

She nods, sipping her drink. "You guys get a lot of rockslides around here?"

I grunt. "Rockslides around here aren't usually that big. The odd one takes a day or two to clear. The end of spring, beginning of the summer is the worst for them, when the snow is melting and the rain is pouring down. Makes the rock faces weak." I glance up at her, seeing her eyes shoot up. "Don't worry, you're safe."

She laughs. "Good." We stare at each other for a moment until she clears her throat and takes another sip of her drink. She looks at me curiously.

"So why the Mad Hatters? Are you a big Lewis Carroll fan?" Her smile twitches.

"No, I just really like hats," I reply. She laughs, and my heart jumps. She shakes her head and throws me a look that makes my cock pulse again. "Nah," I add. "My mom used to read Alice in Wonderland to me when I was a kid. I loved that book, especially the scene with the Mad Hatter. I guess it just fit."

"Makes sense," she says.

"*If I had my own world, everything would be nonsense,*" I say almost automatically.

"*Nothing would be what it is, because everything would be what it isn't.*" Zoe answers. My eyes widen and a laugh tumbles out of me.

"*And contrary wise, what is, it wouldn't be.*"

"*And what it wouldn't be, it would. You see?*" She laughs as she says the last words and shakes her head.

I stare at her, slack-jawed. "I've never met anyone who can quote the Mad Hatter. Not even my own bandmates."

She blushes and stares at her drink. "I played the Mad Hatter in a school play when I was thirteen. It took me ages to learn those lines," she laughs. "I've never forgotten them. Didn't understand them then and still don't understand them now."

"I don't think you're supposed to understand them," I answer with a laugh. "So what are you doing here, anyway? You don't sound like you're local."

She tilts her head to the side and hesitates. She licks her lips and I try not to stare at her, until finally she shrugs.

"Just passing through," she answers. I want to press her, but something in the way she says it makes me think she doesn't want me to ask. "I'm leaving again in the morning, need to go to my new job."

"That's a shame," I reply in a low growl. "It would have been nice to have more than one night together."

Her eyes flash and her grin twitches. "Who said we were having a night together?"

I open my mouth to answer when there's a tap on my shoulder. My drummer, Billy, is glancing from me to Zoe with an unimpressed look on his face.

"We're on. Unless you're too busy...?" He glances at Zoe, who blushes again. The color on her cheeks makes the desire coil in my stomach.

"You're a dickhead, Billy," I answer as he grins. I nod to the stage and start heading toward it when I turn around. I see Zoe slinging her bag over her shoulder and I frown.

"You're leaving?"

"I have an early morning tomorrow," she explains. We look at each other for a few moments and she leans against the bar. Impulsively, I take a step toward her, putting my hand on her waist and brushing my lips over her cheek. She trembles, and my cock pulses again.

"Don't leave before I'm done," I say softly into her ear. I pull away and watch as she wets her lips.

"Is that another rule of yours?" Zoe asks with an eyebrow raised.

"No."

"Okay... I'll stay," she says in a low voice. We stare at each other for a few moments and I finally tear myself away. I look for her when I get on stage and smile when I see her at the bar, sitting in my seat.

3

———

ZOE

I KNOW I SHOULD LEAVE. Even though I'll be working in Lang Creek, a hundred or so miles south of here, it still feels like I shouldn't jump into bed with a strange man on my first night in the Adirondacks. It's not professional, and it sets the wrong tone. The responsible thing to do, as a single mother and newcomer in this area, is to stay professional and leave.

That's the responsible thing to do, but I'm not feeling responsible tonight. How would anyone in Lang Creek even find out? It's a two- or three-hour drive. It might as well be a different universe. How fast can news travel around here?

I nod to the bartender and he pours me another drink as I settle onto my seat — Ethan's seat. My cheeks are still flushed and my heart is still thumping from that conversation, with my cheek burning where his lips brushed it. All I can manage to do is to look at the stage and watch Ethan perform.

I can enjoy the anonymity for a little while longer before I drive down to Lang Creek tomorrow. For now, I'm just a single woman in a bar, enjoying the attention of a very attractive lead singer.

Sure, he's the lead singer of a tiny three-piece band in a tiny little town in the mountains, but it still counts, right?

He meets my eye as he sings and my heart does a backflip. The heat between my legs is still burning, and all I want is for him to press me up against the wall and take me right now. I wonder what it would feel like to have his huge, muscular body pressing against mine, to feel the heat of his breath on my neck and his hips grinding against mine.

I watch his hands move up and down the guitar and I wonder what they would feel like on my body. His fingers might sink into my flesh and he would pull me close to him. I would feel his cock against me, even through our clothing.

I close my eyes for a moment and try to imagine what it would feel like to run my hand up and down the length of his shaft. My center is pulsing, like there's a ball of fire in the pit of my stomach. I haven't been this turned on in far, far too long. I haven't had sex with a man since Mark died. Six years suddenly feels like a long, long, *long* time.

And now? Now I'm about to start a new job in a small town a couple hours' drive from here. I don't know anyone, and I feel more relaxed than I have in years. I'm out on my own, enjoying the attention of an incredibly sexy man. I watch his biceps bulge against his t-shirt as he grabs the microphone, his blue eyes burning into me. Is it possible to pass out from arousal?

As my body continues to heat up, and Ethan continues to look me up and down, a small voice gets louder and louder inside my head.

Why not?

Why not have a night of fun? Why not spend the night with him, and feel the touch of a man again? Why not relax and enjoy myself?

Almost as soon as the final note is played, Ethan turns to his bandmates and hands one of them his guitar. The drummer glances over at me and shrugs before grinning at Ethan. My cheeks burn, but then in a moment Ethan is beside me.

"You want to get out of here?"

"What about your gear? Don't you have to pack up?" I ask as I watch the other men on stage. Ethan grins, sliding his hand to the small of my back.

"They'll manage without me tonight." His eyes flash and my whole body trembles. The warmth of his hand on my back is distracting and intoxicating. All I want to do is melt into his arms and inhale the musky smell of his body. I want to feel his hands all over me and taste his lips. I want to touch his cock and feel him inside me.

I haven't been attracted to a man in so long that I've forgotten what it feels like. I can hardly think straight. I nod to Ethan and he leads me out of the bar. The air is cold, and I lift the collar on my jacket up.

"It's freezing out here!" I exclaim.

Ethan chuckles. "Where did you say you were from? This is pretty warm for this time of year."

I grin. "I'm from Seattle," I answer. "But still, this *isn't* warm."

"West coast, hey," he says, almost under his breath. He slips his hand into mine and guides me down the street. "What are you doing over here? You said you took a job in this area?"

For some reason, I don't want him to know who I am. I don't want to tell him about my life back home, or my daughter, or my job. I just want to be someone else for one night. I don't want to have the problems and burdens of my regular life. I just want to feel the touch of his skin against mine and feel young again. I want to go back to his place and have mind-blowing sex, and then pack up my things and leave in the morning.

If he knows who I am, he can find me again, and then things just get messy. I have to go into a new work environment and assert myself. I don't want to be branded as anything but professional. How am I supposed to be Lang Creek's new fire safety consultant if they know I jumped into bed as soon as the plane landed? It's hard enough making it in this industry as a woman, let alone a single mother who's coming in to teach veterans of the job how to implement new procedures.

So, when Ethan asks me what I'm doing here, I hesitate. I let my lips curl upwards and shrug as my hand traces over his shoulder.

"I don't want to talk about work," I reply. I look up at him through my lashes and bite my lip. "Like you said, we only have one night together. Why waste our breath on things that don't matter?"

Ethan's eyes flash and I see pure, unadulterated desire in them. He wraps his arms around my waist and pulls me close. I fall against him as his hands slide down to my ass. His head dips down toward me and his chest rumbles against me.

"Who are you," he growls. Somehow it doesn't seem like a question. "You just appeared here, out of nowhere."

I curl my fingers into the hair at the nape of his neck. My whole body is shaking and when his hand cups my ass, I feel like I might climax right there in the middle of the road. His body is warm, almost hot. The desire pulsing through my body is making me dizzy. When he stares at me with those icy blue eyes of his, I want him so badly that a whimper escapes my lips and I tremble in his arms.

He growls again, and finally crushes his lips against mine. His hand squeezes my ass as his other hand tangles into my hair. He tilts my head back so that my mouth opens wider as he kisses me harder. I moan, wrapping my arms around him as my panties soak through.

He's strong, but his touch is soft. He kisses me hungrily and growls as his hands explore my body. His hand squeezes my ass again and then brushes up under my shirt to rest on the small of my back. The feeling of his skin on mine makes my head spin. I melt against him, feeling the smooth, hard muscles of his chest as my breasts press up against him.

When he growls again, I pant and pull away. My hands are still on his shoulders, and I look up at him. I know my cheeks are flushed and my chest is heaving up and down. It takes a few seconds for me to speak, and when I do, my voice is scratchy and low.

"Where's your place?" I ask. Ethan smiles and dips his chin down to nod. He grabs my hand in his and points his chin down the road.

"This way," he says, and the two of us walk down the moonlit street as the heat of our desire carries us forward.

4

ETHAN

THE SECOND SATURDAY of the month is usually just 'me' time. I make some excuse to leave Lang Creek, if I happen to run into my brothers. I drive off with my gear in back of my truck and for a few hours, I'm not Ethan Clarke. I'm not Dominic and Aiden's little brother. I'm not a Park Ranger.

For a few hours, I'm the lead singer of the Mad Hatters.

Usually, that's where it ends. I play some music with my buddies, I drink a few beers, and I drive back to Lang Creek in the morning. I think my brothers understand that I want some time away from the town, so they let me leave in peace. A couple times a month we'll play at Harold's Pub in Lang Creek, but my time in this place is my own time.

I just come to Long Lake and play, and then I go back to my regular life.

But this time? This time is different. This time, I've got a gorgeous, sexy, sensual woman who wants me. I can see it in her eyes, and I can feel it in the touch of her hand. I can taste it in her kiss.

She *wants* me.

And fuck, I want her too. We're almost jogging down the street toward my hotel. My hand drops to her back and I run my fingers over her ass. She glances up at me through her lashes and the pulsing between my legs intensifies.

I guide Zoe down the street toward my hotel. I always stay in the same place — Mickey's BnB. Mickey reserves the cabin at the far edge of the property for me, so that I still feel like I'm in the middle of the mountains even when I come to Long Lake.

We stumble back toward my room, passing my truck along the way. Zoe points to the black pickup with her thumb. "Nice wheels. I'm starting to regret getting a car. Seems like everyone has a truck around here."

"Thanks," I say with a grin. "When it gets to winter, you'll understand why everyone has a truck."

"I won't be here for winter," she replies right away, and a pang of disappointment surprises me. I nod.

"Right."

When I lead Zoe to the back of the property, she glances over at me.

"Where are you taking me?" She raises an eyebrow and I grin.

"My room. It's just out back."

"Under different circumstances, I'd be nervous about all this."

I slow down and look at her. "You're not nervous, are you?" Suddenly, I'm worried. What if she isn't joking? I'm dragging her back to a tiny, secluded cabin. She doesn't know me at all. "We don't have to go here if you don't want to. We can go to your place, or back to the bar."

I stop, letting my hand drift to her waist. Zoe chuckles and brushes her fingers over my cheek. She brushes my hair off my forehead and shakes her head. "Stop it," she says. "Although I appreciate that you're a gentleman." Her hands hook around my neck as she presses her lithe body into me. I groan and kiss her again, sinking my fingers into her body as I feel my veins turn to fire.

Panting, I pull away. "You're driving me wild," I say. I see her eyes darken with desire and a smile floats over her lips.

"That makes two of us."

We get to my door and I look through my pockets for my keys. I look at her, shaking my head. The moonlight is making her look almost ethereal. Zoe puts her hands on my chest and pushes me up against the door. My heart is hammering against my ribcage, and she parts her lips as I lean down to taste them again.

We kiss more slowly this time. I wrap my arms around her body and she tangles her fingers into my hair. She presses her body against mine and I can feel her pulse quickening. By the time we separate, she looks up at me and shakes her head.

"I'm not nervous about anything," she answers. "Now take me inside and fuck me, will you?"

My hands are shaking when I try to get the key in the door. Why did I even lock it? It's not like I have anything to steal in here. The key finally slides in the door and we tumble inside.

In an instant, her hands are tearing at my clothes. She's pushing me back toward the bed and ripping my shirt over my head. I fall back onto the bed and she falls on top of me, laughing. I roll her onto her back and straddle my legs over hers, lifting myself up on my forearm and helping her take her shirt off. I run my hand up her stomach and watch her lips part as she lets out a sigh.

I trail my hand over her breast and pull her bra down to thumb her nipple. It stands up, a little hard bud that I can't resist tasting. She groans and bats her eyelashes at me, running her hands up my chest.

"Do you work out?" she asks, tracing my shoulders with her fingers.

"A little," I grin. "I've got an active job."

"Oh yeah?" she says, running her hands over my shoulders some more. She closes her eyes as I twirl my thumb over her nipple again, pressing her nails ever so slightly into my flesh. I groan and press my hips against hers. I don't want to talk about my job. I don't want to talk about working out, or anything else. I just want to plunge the entire length of my shaft inside her and watch her body arch in response. I want those lips to part and I want to hear her gasp.

I'm throbbing. She lifts her hips up toward me and grinds them in slow circles, biting her lip and looking at me.

"You're so fucking sexy," I growl.

Zoe digs her fingers into the back of my neck and I crush my lips against hers. I kiss her harder and harder, tasting her lush lips and gripping her body against mine. My pre-cum is soaking through my boxers and I feel like I'm going to explode.

She's panting, and grabbing, and groping. She tears her bra off and I dive down to run my tongue over her hard nipples. I pull at her jeans, dragging them down her legs and covering her stomach and thighs with more kisses. When I get to her underwear, Zoe's chest is heaving and she's running her hands over and back through my hair.

I grin, and run a finger gently over her panties. The heat of her desire is making me crazy, and I kiss the little pink bow at the front of her underwear. I run my hand between her legs and feel her wetness soaking through the thin fabric. She sighs and pulls her underwear off, shaking her head.

"I can't wait any longer, Ethan," she pants. "Get a condom. Fuck me. Now."

5

ZOE

WHEN HE ENTERS ME, my whole body contracts. I watch the muscles of his chest and stomach ripple as he pushes himself deeper inside me, inch by inch. I'm no longer in control, and all I can do is just ride wave after wave of pleasure. He pinches my nipple and I gasp, arching my back and pushing my hips toward him. He thrusts himself deeper inside me and I gasp again.

It's not what I expected to happen. I doubt it's what my mother had in mind when she told me to go out for a drink, but here I am. I'm fucking the most gorgeous man I've ever seen. The pressure in the pit of my stomach is building as my orgasm starts to bud. I focus on that pinprick of light as the warmth starts to spread to my thighs and my stomach, seeping into my veins and setting my body on fire.

Ethan knows it. He can feel me inching closer and closer to the edge and he plunges himself deeper inside me. He leans over and crushes his lips against mine, driving his cock inside me harder.

I gasp and moan as we grind together. The warmth inside me is spreading. Ethan's eyelids are low. He growls and my body trembles.

"Where did you come from?" He says, his voice rumbling through me. I run my fingers up his chest in response, and he wraps his arms around my back. He lifts me up and drives his cock deeper inside me as his other hand slips between us to find my bud.

He grinds himself into me as I wrap my legs around him. My nails leave long, red scratch marks down his back as I throw my head back with a silent scream. His fingers twirl around my bud as he pushes his shaft a little bit deeper into me, and the pinprick of light in my stomach becomes a burning inferno.

I find my voice as the waves of pleasure start rolling over me. The ecstasy is rippling through my body like never before, and I feel his length inside me as if it belongs there. I squeeze my legs around him, sinking my nails into his skin as he grunts, biting my shoulder gently.

He moans with me as I arch my back and let myself go. His body tenses in my arms as the orgasm rips through my body. I can feel every movement he makes, hear every noise he utters, sense every bit of his body against mine as we hold on to each other. I feel his pleasure as viscerally as my own, and we come together. His hands sink into my body and I melt into him as our bodies fuse together.

I ride wave after wave of pleasure as my body trembles and shakes with him. He's panting, his mouth near my ear so I can feel the heat of his breath on my neck. He's lying on top of me, with his chest against mine. Our skin is sweaty, and the air in the room is thick and heady.

Ethan groans and rolls to his side. I turn toward him and drape my arm across his chest. He runs his fingers over and back along my forearm, and we fall into a dreamy post-coital daze.

I doze off at one point, waking up when Ethan moves. He moans, opening his eyes and glancing over at me.

"I think I fell asleep," he says.

"Me too," I reply as a smile plays across my lips. "How long did we sleep?"

Ethan glances at his clock and shakes his head. "Couple minutes. Feels like hours." He turns back toward me and the corner of his lip twitches upwards. "That was nice."

I nod, and Ethan turns toward me. He reaches over and tucks a strand of hair behind my ear. He smiles and traces the line of my jaw with his finger.

"You're beautiful," he breathes.

My voice catches in my throat. Something in the way he's looking at me makes my heart thump. We stay like that for a few moments, and then he moves toward me to kiss me gently. His lips brush over mine, and his arm wraps around my back. My body is still buzzing from my orgasm, and every touch is electrifying.

He pulls me closer and we make love again. This time it's slower, but my orgasm is just as intense. By the time we're finished, my legs are shaking and I feel completely spent. I fall asleep with my arms and legs tangled with his.

. . .

WHEN THE SUN starts poking over the horizon, I wake up with a start. Ethan groans and shifts beside me, but doesn't quite wake up. His lips are parted and he's snoring gently. I trace my hand over his stubble and along his jaw.

He's gorgeous.

He could be a model. Even with his hair sticking up all over the place and his mouth hanging open, he still looks like he walked straight out of the pages of a magazine. I glance down his body, watching his muscular chest rise and fall with every breath. His cock is twitching under the sheet, and my thighs start to warm right away. I drop my hand to his chest and trace every muscle with my fingertips. I run my fingers all over him, back and forth, lower and lower until I get to the length between his legs.

As soon as my hand touches him, he groans and opens his eyes.

"Good morning to you, too," he grunts with a smile. Ethan closes his eyes and takes a deep breath, letting it out with a groan. "I could think of worse ways to wake up."

I'm already slick with desire. I fumble for a condom, my hands trembling as I slip it on. I climb up on top of him and slide down onto his shaft. He gasps, opening his eyes wider and gripping my thighs with his strong hands.

I can't get enough of him. My body is on fire, and the only thing I can do is give in to my urges. My body is sore and tired from our night together, but it doesn't matter. We ride and thrust and moan and scream until the room smells like sweat and sex. I collapse on top of him and enjoy the last quivers of my orgasm.

I lay my head on his chest, listening to the beating of his heart slow down as we lie motionless. His fingers are trailing up and down my spine and he brushes the hair off my forehead, laying a kiss on my skin and grunting.

"Sweaty," he says, wiping his lips. I laugh.

"Sorry."

I look up at him and smile. His eyes are gleaming, and he runs his fingers along my temple and through my hair.

This wasn't what I was expecting when I went out last night, but somehow, it was exactly what I needed. I'm calmer and more relaxed than I've been in months. I peel myself away and kiss him gently one more time.

"I should go," I whisper. He pulls me closer and kisses me, nuzzling his head into my neck.

"Don't go," he says. "It's Sunday. Stay until tonight. Surely you don't have to be anywhere until tomorrow?"

I smile as my heart squeezes. *I wish I could.* I think of Audrey, and my mother, and my new job, and I shake my head. I need to get down to Lang Creek to get organized before my first day. Sleeping with a gorgeous man to let off some steam is one thing, but staying here to see him is quite another. I can't let distractions get in the way of what's important.

"I have to go," I reply. "Can I use your shower?" I drag myself away again and laugh when he pouts.

"At least let me take your number."

I hesitate. I want to give it to him. I want to see him again. Every fiber of my being is screaming at me to stay, to give him my number, to spend the day eating and fucking and laughing with him.

The responsible voice in my head finally wins. I smile at him and run my finger along his temple, giving his scalp a soft massage.

"I want to," I start.

"But...?" He raises an eyebrow.

"But let's just leave it where we are," I reply. "I'll be gone soon. It's easier this way." Too many distractions will make me forget why I'm here. I need to finish training the Parks staff, and I can't become involved romantically with anyone, even if they don't live in the same town as me.

Especially if he lives far away. I can't waste any time or energy on anything except getting this project going and getting back to my daughter.

Ethan is hurt, I can tell. He drops his eyes and his body stiffens. He nods.

"Yeah," he answers. His voice has an edge that I haven't heard before. "You're right. It's simpler this way."

"Think of it this way," I say as I pull away from him and swing my legs off the bed. "I'm your first groupie. There'll be thousands of girls like me when your band hits it big." I find my jeans, inside out and flung over the dresser in our haste last night.

He chuckles. "I don't know if anyone can top the night we just had, though."

My heart squeezes and I glance at him. I know he means it, and it scares me. I purse my lips into a thin line and pull on the rest of my clothes, glancing around the room to make sure I have everything.

"Thanks for a great night," I say as I lean into the bed and kiss him again. He reaches up and runs his fingers around the nape of my neck, pulling me in for a deeper kiss. His other hand reaches toward my waist.

Before I know it, he's pulling me down beside him and rolling on top of me. I giggle and yelp as he covers my neck in kisses.

"Ethan!" I protest, laughing and loving the way he's worshipping my body.

He lifts his head up and his eyes are full of mischief. "One more time," he growls. "For the road."

My smile twitches and I dip my chin down. "One for the road," I repeat. His grin widens and he crushes his lips against mine before tearing the clothes off my body once more.

6

ETHAN

BY THE TIME ZOE LEAVES, I'm exhausted. My body feels completely empty, and I don't know what to think. I let out a sigh and fold my arms behind my head as I lay down in bed. I look at the ceiling of my little log cabin, tracing the grain of the wooden slats above me with my eyes.

I can't believe I met a woman like that in a town like this, and I can't believe I couldn't get her number. On the one hand, I understand. She's just passing through, and she wanted to acknowledge last night for what it was: one night of fun.

'Fun' seems like the wrong word. It was passion. It was the hottest sex I've had in my life. She ran her hands over my body as if she was trying to memorize it. She wrapped her legs around me and fucked me like no other woman I've been with.

And then, she left.

I sigh and close my eyes to remember her kiss. I try to freeze the memory of her in my mind, so that I can remember last night for a long time. I don't want to forget what it felt like to be with a woman like that, to have her give herself over to me so completely.

As much as I understand why she doesn't want to keep seeing me, rejection stings. I get it, but my ego is bruised. Was last night as good for her as it was for me? Did she enjoy it? It felt like an almost out-of-body experience for me. When I came, it was like my whole body was screaming at once, like every nerve in my body was firing together.

And she came too. I *know* she did. I could feel it, and I could see it in her face. I know she felt what I felt. I could see the hunger in her eyes this morning. Her body was like a coiled spring. Feeling that energy release was intoxicating. And yet... she still wanted to leave and never see me again?

I blow the air out of my nostrils and swing my legs over the side of the bed. I shake my head and run my fingers through my hair.

I'm being ridiculous and insecure. Somehow, in less than twenty-four hours, Zoe got under my skin and shook me off balance. Isn't it usually the *guy* that leaves in the morning and never calls back? Shouldn't it be *me* who's the heartbreaker here?

It's unusual for me to feel this way. I'm used to having women chase *me*, not the other way around.

I stand up and head toward the shower. The thoughts are crashing around in my head, and I step under the stream of water to try to wash my body and mind clean. I scrub myself thoroughly and then just stand under the water with my eyes closed and my mouth open.

By the time I step back out of the shower, I'm calmer. I got fired up by a sexy woman, but she's right. It's better this way. I gather my things and check out of the hotel. I might as well head back to Lang Creek before dark. I have to work in the morning, after all.

When I get to the front desk, Mickey is sitting down watching an old TV show. He glances up when I walk in and grins.

"Looks like you had a good night," he chirps.

I shrug, ignoring his unsaid question. "It was alright."

Mickey barks a laugh and takes the room keys. "Book you in for next month?" He asks.

I nod. "Same time, same room. You know it."

"See you then, buddy."

Mickey nods at me and I walk out of the hotel's office, heading toward my pickup truck. I load it up with my gear and clothes, and then slide in behind the wheel and make my way onto the freeway. I glance in my rear-view mirror as Long Lake disappears behind me, and I shake my head.

I don't want to tell my brothers about her, or anyone in Lang Creek. I want to keep the memory of last night buried deep inside me and hope that somehow, I'll run into Zoe again.

By the time I make it to Lang Creek, the sun is getting lower. I slow down as I make my way through the town, heading toward my little cabin on the edge of the forest. It's a quiet, sleepy place, and for the first time in a long time, I feel restless.

My thoughts keep drifting back to Zoe and our night together. I think of her laugh and the way her eyes sparkled when I touched her. How could I ever find a woman like that in a tiny town like Lang Creek? It doesn't help that I spend days on my own in the Park.

When I park my truck in front of my house, I lean back in the driver's seat and close my eyes for an instant. I have to snap out of it. She's gone, and I'll probably never see her again. We had a great night together, and I should appreciate that. That's all it was: one night.

I jump when someone knocks on the car window, and then relax when I see my brother.

"Hey, Dominic," I say as I open the door.

"How was the show?" he asks. He's a couple inches taller than me and built like a football player. His eyes narrow as he watches me grab my bag from the passenger's seat before getting out of the car. "I came by last night and you weren't here, forgot it was the second Saturday of the month."

"Are you tracking all my movements now?" I ask with a grin. There's an edge to my voice that even I can hear. Dominic frowns and then shakes his head.

"Whatever, man. I brought you that table you wanted." I follow my brother as he leads me to his truck, and I leave the memory of last night behind me. I'm back in Lang Creek, and back to work tomorrow. Things are exactly as they were before this weekend. All I did was meet a woman and sleep with her.

Still, as Dominic and I bring my new table inside, something feels different. I hand my brother a beer and we sink down on my couch, but we don't speak to each other. He glances at me a few times and then finally stands up, putting a hand on my shoulder as he walks by.

"I'm going home," he grunts. "Take care of yourself."

I nod at him. When the door closes behind him, I lean back in the sofa and let out a sigh. Something has changed, and I'm not sure it's a good thing.

7

ZOE

THE ALARM IS BLARING, and I smack my arm down over the bedside table to try to turn it off. I miss, and the alarm keeps beeping. It's an old alarm clock, with bright red numbers and a long snooze bar. I crawl my fingers over the bedside table until I find the alarm clock and turn it off.

I groan into my pillow before opening one eye and looking at the clock: 5:30am. It's early, but it's just enough time to go for an early morning run before work. I sigh and roll out of bed. My eyes are still mostly closed as I head to my stack of workout clothes. Thankfully, I left everything out and ready for the morning. I'm not sure I'd have the energy or the drive to dig through my suitcases for running leggings. I pull them on, still half-asleep.

It takes me about a mile before I'm truly awake. My head-phones are blaring in my ears and I can see the first rays of sunshine coming out over the mountains. I'm at the edge of town, and there's a thick mist hanging low on the ground. The air is crisp and clean. When I inhale, I remember why I like to get up this early.

By the time the sun is warming the ground, I'm turning back toward the town of Lang Creek. I wind my way through the trails that I've been running on, and head back toward the main road. As I leave the forest behind me, a black pickup truck catches my eye. I slow down, frowning.

My heart starts beating harder as I get closer to it. It's parked outside a single-story house. Well, a cabin, really. Most of the houses in this town are log cabins.

I stare at the truck, reading the license plate and trying to remember the truck parked outside Ethan's BnB. When I pass it, I shake my head and continue toward the town. I ignore the thumping in my heart, blaming my run for the hammering in my chest.

It's probably not his. How many people around here have black pickup trucks? Probably everyone in town, and everyone in the next town, and the next. I shake my head, taking a deep breath and trying to forget the smell of his skin and the touch of his hands on my body. It was one night, and I'm probably never going to see him again.

And even if the truck *was* his, who cares? So he lives in Lang Creek! What does that change? We had one night of fun. I thought I'd never see him again, but even if I do see him, it doesn't mean we have to date.

Still, my heart is still racing and I know it's not because I'm running. A deep well of excitement starts to build inside me when I think of seeing him again. What if it *was* his truck? I might run into him at the grocery store, or at the bar. We could talk, and maybe even grab a drink together. And then... well, whatever happens, happens.

As I get to my hotel, I climb the steps up to my room and close the door behind me. I lean on it, closing my eyes and sighing. My blood is pumping and my breath is heavy, and all I can think of is Ethan.

Even if he lives here, seeing him again would be a bad idea. A *terrible* idea! I'd be the new girl in town, immediately crawling into bed with one of the locals. Bad, bad idea.

I open my eyes again and try to forget about him. There's no way that was his truck. I'm just riled up because I've had sex for the first time in years. I'd probably be infatuated with anyone at this point.

I peel my sweaty running clothes off and jump in the shower. I stand under the water and try to wash off the thoughts of Ethan swirling in my head. I start a new job today, and I need to focus. I'm all over the place! Even the sight of a generic black pickup truck is sending me reeling.

I wash myself methodically, enjoying the billowing steam and the hot water of the shower. When I wash between my legs, a tiny thrill passes through me. I pause, and remember the way Ethan was touching me just twenty-four hours ago. My fingers move in slow circles, and I remember the way his breath was heavy in my ear. I remember his groans, and the way he grunted when he came. I remember his lips crushed against mine, and his hands all over my body.

The water is pouring down over me and I put a hand on the shower wall to steady myself. I'm panting again, and my fingers are moving faster and faster. When I come, I'm thinking of him. My body is shaking and I can hardly hold myself up, but I manage to turn off the shower and steady myself.

As I dry myself off with a thick white towel, I sigh. I wrap the towel around me and fall into bed, closing my eyes for a moment and groaning in satisfaction.

Even if it wasn't Ethan's truck parked in Lang Creek, I'm still getting some good mileage out of the thought of him.

I can't enjoy the after-effects of my orgasm, because my phone rings. I drag myself out of bed and see my daughter's face on my phone. I press the green button to answer, and a video call starts between us.

"Morning, Mom!" Audrey says. She has a huge smile on her face and I gasp.

"Your tooth!"

Audrey laughs. "I lost it this morning! Grandma says if I put it under my pillow, the tooth fairy will come and give me a dollar." She glances behind her and comes closer to the camera. "But I know the tooth fairy doesn't exist."

"How do you know that?" I ask, my heart squeezing as I realize my little girl is growing up.

"Megan at school told me."

"Ah, well don't listen to everything Megan tells you."

"She told me that I look ugly with my missing tooth," Audrey says, and I see a flash of pain across her face. My heart squeezes again and I wish I were there to give her a hug.

"That was very mean of Megan," I say, frowning. "You know you're beautiful, Audrey, don't you?"

Audrey makes a noise and doesn't look at me. I frown again. "Is Megan mean to you often, Audrey?"

My daughter takes a deep breath and won't look at the camera. I frown and sit up, holding the towel up on my chest.

Audrey shrugs and shuffles the phone in her hand. She shows me her tooth, turning it around in her hand and laughing. I smile, and my heart grows in my chest. We talk for a few minutes, and then she puts my mother on.

"Hey, Mom," I say. "Did Audrey mention this Megan girl to you?"

My mom's lips purse and I see her face cloud. She nods. "Doesn't sound like a very nice girl. I've tried talking to Audrey about it but she gets really quiet when I try to press her."

"I hope she's not being bullied."

"I'll try to talk to her. How was your weekend? Did you go out for a drink on Saturday?"

"Yeah," I reply. "It was nice."

My mom nods, and I hear Audrey in the background. "I'd better let you go," my mom says. "Love you, Zoe."

"Love you too, Mom," I reply.

We hang up the phone and I hold it to my chest. Yes, I've been lonely since Mark died, and yes, I loved Ethan's attention. But at the end of the day, I'm here for my daughter. I'm making some money that will pay for her piano and soccer and start a small college fund for her. The next couple months working on this contract are important for me and most importantly, for my daughter.

I sigh and put my phone aside, rubbing my eyes and combing my fingers through my hair. I get up and finish getting ready.

By the time I'm getting in my rental car, I've put all thoughts of Ethan aside. I'm going to go to the Ranger's Station and start Day One of their new training. I'll do the best possible job I can, and I'll bring home a great paycheck for my daughter's future.

Those words play back over and over in my mind until I pull up outside the Station. I feel calm, and confident, and focused. I'm ready to do this, even if it'll be difficult.

When I get out of my car and head toward the small, green building, I catch a glimpse of a pickup truck parked on the side of the building. It's the same one I saw this morning. I frown, and my heart starts beating faster. I keep walking toward the building, and grab the door handle with one hand. I glance at the black pickup one more time, and then pull open the door and step through.

8

———

ETHAN

"So, who is she?" Bryan asks as I pour myself a hot cup of coffee.

"What?" I ask, glancing at him. "What are you talking about?"

He leans against the staff room counter and raises an eyebrow before shaking his head and chuckling. "Ethan, I've known you since you were four. I know the look you get when you've just gotten laid."

My eyebrows shoot up and I try to look as innocent as possible. "What?"

Bryan laughs. "Was it Katie? She's been wanting you since we were teenagers. Did you finally go for it?"

"Fuck off, Bryan," I laugh, turning my back to him to hide my face. "Maybe I just had a good night's sleep!"

He snorts and pushes himself off the counter. "Fine. If you don't want to share, that's fine. But you'll tell me eventually." He nods to the main office. "You ready for this new consultant today? Should be a fun couple months of someone new telling us how to do our jobs."

"Ugh," I groan. "I don't see the point. We'll just have to pretend to care what he says and go through this bullshit training. I can tell you for sure that there won't be any more buildings burning down around here."

Bryan laughs. The whole town knows that it was me, my brother, and Sheriff Whittaker that burned down the luxury hotel under construction last year. We did it to protect the town against the inevitable onslaught of tourists, and to prevent the McCoy family from owning the entire town. We have no plans of becoming full-time arsonists.

"One-time thing, hey?" Bryan chuckles. "Here I thought you were some badass vigilante."

"Well, as long as a corporate hotel developer doesn't try to set up shop here again, then yeah," I grin. "It's a waste of time and money, getting this consultant in." *And the last thing I need is someone digging up the past. The town might be supportive of the fire, but it doesn't mean it was legal.*

Bryan grunts and we head out toward the main room. Sandy is at her desk, with her hair tied into her usual tight bun at the nape of her neck and stern look on her face. She glances at Bryan and me and slides her glasses down to the tip of her nose.

"You two look like you're up to something," she says.

I shake my head. "Nothing, boss. Don't worry. Just getting excited for this training."

I guess my voice was a bit more sarcastic than I meant it to be, because Sandy stands up and puts her hands on her wide hips. She's an imposing woman, standing almost as tall as me and just as strong. She takes a step toward me and raises a finger at me.

"Don't you cause any trouble, Ethan Clarke. I know you think this training is bogus, but it's compulsory. The Department mandated it after the fire."

I sigh. "Sandy–"

She raises an eyebrow and I stop talking. My shoulders slump and I nod. "I'll do the training."

"Good. Now go get the conference room ready, we'll have a meeting when she gets here."

"She? I thought it was supposed to be a man."

Sandy snorts. "If I had a nickel for every time someone assumed I was a man before meeting me, I'd be a very rich woman. No, Ethan," she says as she looks at and snorts. "Zoe Randall is the best safety consultant in the country, and she is most definitely a *woman*."

"Zoe," I repeat. My chest feels hollow and my eyes widen as I look at my boss. She frowns, and I feel frozen in place.

Could it be Zoe... *my* Zoe? The one from this weekend? The one that I thought I'd never see again? My heart starts thumping and a flurry of emotions washes over me. The thrill of excitement at seeing her again, and the sting of rejection mixed with the undeniable buzz of arousal.

Just then, the front door opens and everything moves in slow motion. I can feel every muscle in my neck as I turn my head. Every hair on my body is standing on end, and Sandy's voice seems to reach my ears a moment too late.

My head is spinning. It can't be her. There's something wrong. My mind is playing tricks on me. If it *is* her, then we'll be working together for the foreseeable future. I turn toward the door, and her body is silhouetted in the doorway. Her hair is tied back in a sleek ponytail, and she's wearing thick Parks uniform pants and a tight top. My eyes roam over her body and my mouth goes dry.

Images flash through my mind. I see her on top of me, with her mouth falling open as she orgasms. I see the animalistic desire that burned through her when I first entered her. I see her body, naked and gleaming in the soft glow of my cabin at Long Lake.

And now she's here. At my work. In my town. Poking her nose into the fire that *I* started.

"Zoe?" I say, but it comes out as a croak.

She looks just as shocked as I feel. She's frozen in the doorway, mouth agape as she stares at me. We stay there, motionless, for what seems like an eternity. Part of me wants to run to her and wrap my arms around her and taste her kiss again and again, and another part of me wants to run far, far away.

She's the safety consultant?! *She's* the one who will be snooping around my life and my town?!

My heart is thumping, and it's not until Sandy clears her throat that I snap out of it.

"Do you two know each other?"

Zoe jumps at the sound of Sandy's voice and turns toward her, painting a watery smile on her face. She shakes her head. "No," she answers, turning toward me. "I'm Zoe Randall."

A pain passes through my chest when she says those words. *No,* she said. She doesn't know me. A hot flash of anger passes through me and then dissipates when I see the pleading look in her eye.

I know it's better this way. I know better than anyone how vicious the rumors in this town can be. It would be a disaster for her, too, to start working here with that kind of gossip following her.

Of course it's better for us to pretend that Saturday night never happened. But still, it stings. Zoe extends her hand toward me and I clear my throat.

"Ethan," I reply, taking her hand in mine. Her touch feels electric, and my cock throbs as I shake her hand. Even the touch of her skin sends a thrill through me. She swallows, and my eyes drift over the soft curve of her lips. She glances to Sandy and pulls her hand away. As soon as she moves away from me, she doesn't look at me again. Her eyes avoid mine, and I stand in the middle of our office, stunned.

The air seems colder, and I can hardly focus. I stumble toward the bathroom and push the door in as the rest of them exchange pleasantries. I lock the door and turn on the tap to splash water over my face.

It takes me a few minutes to come back to myself. I stare at my face in the mirror, watching the droplets of water fall off my chin, and I grab some paper towels.

She's *here.* She's working with me.

This is either the best thing that's ever happened or the absolute worst. Judging by her face and the stiffness in her shoulders when she saw me, she seems to be leaning toward 'absolute worst'. I dry my face and toss the brown paper towels in the trash, square my shoulders and walk back out toward the main office.

It might be the absolute worst thing that's ever happened, but it's happening whether I like it or not.

9

———

ZOE

ONCE THE SHOCK WEARS OFF, the panic sets in. Has he told anyone? *Will* he tell anyone?

I'm supposed to be a professional. I'm supposed to have some distance, to be an impartial consultant and advisor. How could I ever do that if I've slept with one of the Park Rangers on the very first night I got here?

No, not just *slept* with a ranger. We tore at each other. We ravaged each other. There was very little sleeping involved.

I can still feel his hands on my body, and the feeling of his shaft buried deep inside me. Even the thought of it sends a shiver through my body. I can feel him watching me, and it's making my whole body burn with desire.

I knew it was a mistake. I knew I wouldn't be able to get away with a night of fun.

Sandy is looking at me over her black-rimmed glasses, which are perched precariously close to the end of her nose. One eyebrow is raised, and she has her hands on her hips. She towers above me and seems to be at least twice as wide.

I'd be lying if I said she wasn't intimidating.

"So, Ms. Randall, welcome to our little town."

She's still studying me, and I nod and clear my throat. "Call me Zoe, please," I start. Out of the corner of my eye I see Ethan ducking out of the room, and the tension inside me eases ever so slightly. "It's great to finally be here."

"We've set up the conference room for you. We'll have a short staff meeting to bring you up to speed with what we have done since the fire. You can assess the steps that have been taken over the past year to make sure this doesn't happen again. I'm assuming you've gotten a full summary of what happened?"

"Well, yes. I know there was a fire, and I know it was deemed to be arson but no charges were brought. Were there any suspects?"

Sandy clears her throat and mercifully takes her gaze off my face. She shuffles some papers on her desk and motions toward the conference room.

"Please," she says. I decide not to press her about the fire. Instead, I follow her into the conference room and wait for the other employees to join us.

The last to arrive is Ethan. He slides in the door and takes a seat on the opposite end of the table to me. He avoids eye contact, choosing instead to play with a pen and keep his eyes glued on the table that separates us. I watch him run his fingers along the wood grain, and the motion of his hand reminds me of the way he touched me. I'm burning for him. This is going to drive me crazy.

My throat tightens and I regret denying that I knew him. Even from the opposite end of the room, I can almost feel the way his body was next to mine. His uniform is dark green, and looks like it was made for him. Every muscle presses out against his uniform, stretching the fabric and reminding me what it felt like to have his arms wrapped around me.

His broad shoulders are slumped, and his hair is falling in ringlets over his temples. I desperately want to touch him. I want to brush his hair back and rub his shoulders. I want to undress him, button by button, until I can see his gorgeous, naked body again.

Sandy clears her throat and I jump. *Have I been staring at him?*

"Thank you all for coming in this morning. I'd like to introduce you to the newest member of our team, Zoe Randall. Ms. Randall will be here for the next three months to consult on our safety and incident response procedures. We don't want a repeat of the hotel fire."

There's a murmur in the room and I look around at the various faces. It's an odd bunch. There's Bryan, the young redhead who keeps stealing glances my way. He's sitting next to Ethan and they seem to know each other quite well.

Then, there's Eddie, the old man who has probably worked for the Parks for multiple decades. His uniform is so worn it looks almost beige now, instead of the pale grey and deep green that the others are wearing. He's leaning back in his chair with his arms crossed over his protruding belly. One button has come undone near his navel, and I can see some long, wiry grey hairs poking out of his shirt.

There are two other women, Meghan and Lisa, about my age, and three other men whose names I don't catch. The conference room is full, and the temperature is rising by the minute in the small, stuffy room.

I look back to Sandy and try to focus on what she's saying.

"We haven't had any rain in three weeks, so we need to be really vigilant about fires. The state has just issued a total fire ban, so when you do your rounds, be on the lookout for campfires or evidence of them."

She points her finger down the long table to Ethan.

"Clarke," she says. He jumps a bit and stands up straighter. He glances at me for a fraction of a second before nodding to Sandy.

"Yes, boss," he says, waiting for her to continue.

"You'll take Ms. Randall out to the old hotel grounds. You know as well as any of us what happened that night."

Bryan and Eddie snort, and I shoot a glance their way. Bryan looks at me and quickly averts his eyes, while Eddie ignores me completely. I glance down at the buttons of his shirt that look dangerously close to popping open and revealing more grey belly hair.

Eddie slaps Ethan on the back. "Best man for the job," he laughs as he stands up.

"Anything else, Sandy?"

"No, that's it. Thanks."

He waddles out the door, taking his stomach hairs with him. I stare at Ethan, who pointedly ignores my gaze. What did Eddie mean? Why would he be the best man for the job?

Has Ethan told them about us? Am I already the laughing-stock of the entire office? He's the best man to show me around since he already knows me so... *intimately.*

My cheeks are burning and my heart is thumping against my ribs. I keep my head down as the team files out of the room, leaving only Ethan, Sandy, and me behind.

"So, Ethan, take Zoe up to the grounds and show her where the fire took place. She'll need a full site walk and a full account of what we know." Sandy pauses, and I glance up at her. She's got her mouth open, as if she's going to speak, but then shakes her head.

"And I'll need the campsite maintenance report for Camp-sites A through G by tomorrow evening."

"No problem," Ethan says, nodding to Sandy. She gathers her things and the meeting is over.

Ethan and I sit still for a few moments, and finally I clear my throat.

"Have you got time to show me the site this morning?"

He swings his eyes toward me and my breath catches in my throat. We hold each other's gaze for a few never-ending seconds. I could cut the air in the room with a knife. If the temperature was rising when the room was full, it's absolutely sweltering in here now. I shift in my seat until he finally nods.

"Let's go," he finally replies. "Ready whenever you are."

10

ETHAN

I'M FINDING it hard to think of anything to say. We get in the black pickup truck without a word, and I start driving toward the old hotel grounds.

Toward the scene of the crime.

My crime.

We ride in silence for a long time. Or at least, it feels like a long time. Finally, Zoe clears her throat.

"So, this is unexpected," she says. "Meeting you here."

I glance over at her, running my eyes down the curve of her neck to her body and then back toward the road. I'm not quite sure how to respond.

"Yeah," I say. "I didn't know you were 'Randall'. I thought it would be a guy."

Zoe chuckles. "That's what everyone calls me back home. I can understand the confusion."

I turn down a narrow gravel road and we bounce along for a few minutes. It's awkward. I glance at Zoe again and then turn toward the road. It's just another half mile up this slope and we'll be getting to the old, burned-down remains of the hotel.

"Why did you say you didn't know me?" The question almost falls out of my mouth almost by accident. I can feel Zoe turn to look at me, and she sighs.

"I'm not sure. I panicked. If we said we knew each other, what would we say? I just... I didn't want to start off like that." I can hear the tension in her voice and a lump forms in my throat.

Before I can respond, we round the last corner and the trees clear. Zoe inhales sharply as I park the truck to the side of the road. She opens the door immediately and I watch her jump down and walk toward the burned-out husk of building. There are small saplings and plants growing all over it, with moss and grass creeping up the rubble. Slowly, the forest is reclaiming the construction site. In a few years it'll be easy to miss.

I follow Zoe and we walk in silence. I watch her climb over old beams and rocks, inspecting burn marks and looking around at the devastation. She turns back toward me and shakes her head.

"This could have turned into a major forest fire," she says. "You guys were lucky."

"It was at the beginning of the summer last year, when everything was wet," I deflect. "It wasn't like it is now."

"Still," she says, picking up a charred piece of wood. "Look at the trees along the edges. You can tell the closest side of them has been damaged."

I glance over toward where she's pointing. She's right. The trees that line the clearing are off-balance, like the branches on this side of them have been stunted.

"I read the police report. It said there were three points of ignition, which means there were at least three people here. Whoever did this were real scumbags," she says, pursing her lips. She kicks a rock out of the way and puts her hands on her hips. "It could have been a disaster."

"Could have been," I answer, trying to keep my voice steady. *Scumbag.* That's not exactly the view I have of myself. "The development would have been much more destructive than the fire," I say. Zoe turns toward me and tilts her head to the side. My eyes dart to her lips, and for an instant I remember what they taste like.

I continue. "It would have brought so many people here that wouldn't respect the forest like we do," I say. She stares at me, her face blank. "If you ask me, the fire was a good thing."

She snorts. "A good thing? Aren't there better —you know, *legal* —ways of opposing these things?"

"Legal?" I say, glancing around the overgrown site of the fire. "What chance does our tiny town have against multi-million dollar investors? Against people, money, and power that don't care about anything except profit?" The anger inside me is rising as I think of Margaret McCoy, the woman who master-minded the whole project. The woman who disappeared when it all blew up in her face.

Zoe surprises me when she agrees. "That's true. But I can't condone arson."

We're quiet for a while, and I watch her walk through the wreckage. I show her the places where the fire started, remembering how it felt to splash gasoline over the ground and strike the match to light it up. Zoe crouches down near the spot where I dropped my match.

"So what happened after the fire?" she asks. "No one's really given me a straight answer. It sounds like it all sort of went away." Her bright blue eyes are boring into me, and I know I have to choose my words carefully. *It all went away because the Sheriff started the fire with us.*

I sigh. "Lang Creek is a funny kind of town. Change isn't really encouraged here."

"But arson is?" she retorts. The corner of her lip is curled up into a grin. I chuckle.

"I guess it is," I answer. "More so than razing a huge swath of virgin forest to develop it, just for tourists to come destroy the land that we've cherished for generations."

"You sound like you agree with the people who burned this down."

My chest tightens. It feels wrong to lie to her, even though I hardly know her. I thought this whole business with the hotel and the fire and the McCoys was over! I thought the town had moved on from the fire, and I wouldn't have to worry about it.

Now there's this woman sniffing around, and I *know* she won't be as forgiving as the Sheriff's office or the townspeople. Sure, she's just here to consult on new safety procedures, but that doesn't mean she couldn't get the authorities to reopen the investigation. I wonder how long it'll take for her to hear the rumors that it was my brothers and me?

"Maybe I do agree with them. I mean, look around," I say, sweeping my arm across the landscape. "The forest is taking over again. If the hotel had been built, this whole area would be filled with people and cars and trucks and noise and garbage."

She makes a noise and nods, looking out at the forest.

She sighs. "It *is* very beautiful up here. You're lucky to have lived here all your life."

I snort. "I'm guessing that's a 'grass is always greener' situation, because I sure didn't love living here when I was a teenager."

She laughs. For the first time since she walked through the office door, she really laughs. She laughs like she did our first night together, like she did in the bar when we didn't know anything about each other.

Zoe is still smiling when she takes a step and loses her footing on some loose rock. She yelps, stumbling. I jump toward her, crossing the few feet of distance between us and lunge to catch her. I just about make it, but instead I land with a thud on the rocky ground with Zoe tumbling on top of me.

"*Unf,*" she groans as she lands on top of me. It takes a couple confused seconds for us to disentangle ourselves from each other. She puts her hand on my chest to lift herself off me, raising her eyes up to mine. She stops and my hand drifts to her waist.

The moment only lasts a second, maybe two, but in her eyes, I see something that she hasn't shown me at all today: *desire*. Her eyes flash, and her body almost trembles on top of me. She parts her lips ever so slightly as her pupils dilate.

I can feel her pulse, and when my hand lands on her waist she makes the tiniest of noises.

Then, the moment is over. She lifts herself off and extends a hand to help me up. She brushes herself off and pats her hair down before blowing the air out of her lungs.

"Wow, I, uh," she says, shaking her head. "Thanks."

I grunt, feeling the spots where a rock dug into my lower back. "I think Sandy would kill me if I let you get injured on your very first trip outdoors."

Zoe laughs. "It doesn't look like it would take much to set her off."

"She's alright," I say, grinning with her. "Tough woman, but a good boss."

Zoe looks over once more at the forest. There's a bird chirping nearby, and the wind rustles gently through the leaves. She takes a deep breath and closes her eyes before turning to me and smiling.

"I like it here," she says.

I'm not sure why, but it makes me feel good to hear her say that. My heart thumps and I nod, clearing my throat and turning back toward the truck.

"That's the site of the fire, anyway. I'll take you back along the old logging roads and show you some of the campsites we have."

Our boots crunch on the gravel as we head back to the car. The breeze sweeps by us and the leaves rustle some more. Another bird starts singing.

My head is spinning. I know I need to be careful with Zoe, for my sake and my brothers'. I know it would be best to keep my distance, to keep her at an arm's length.

But when we slide back into my truck, we fall into a comfortable silence, and despite my best efforts to ignore it, I feel *good* having her beside me.

11

ZOE

BY THE TIME I make it back to the hotel, the tiredness has set into my bones but my mind is buzzing. I still can't believe I'm working with Ethan.

I drop my purse on the small desk near the entrance to the room and sink down on the chair. I close my eyes and enjoy a few moments of silence.

Immediately, my brain starts replaying the day. I see Ethan as he glanced at me sideways in the truck, and the thrill it sent through my whole body. I can feel his hand on my waist and my body pressed against his when I fell. The look in his eyes was nothing short of electrifying.

Shaking my head, I get up and sigh. I stretch my arms above my head and glance around the tiny hotel room that I'm going to call home for the next two to three months. I glance at the picture of Audrey that I've propped on my nightstand, and take a deep breath.

I should forget about Saturday. It was one night, and it meant nothing.

We seem to have an unspoken understanding about that, which simultaneously fills me with relief and a stinging sensation in the center of my chest. It was me who walked away without giving him my number, and it was me who pretended not to know him, so I shouldn't be upset that he's respected my wishes.

I stand still, staring at nothing, until a knock on the door makes me jump.

"Hi," says a young woman when I open the door. She's wearing a hotel uniform and holding a stack of towels. She smiles hesitantly. "Mara sent me over to make sure you had everything you need and to give you these," she says, presenting me with a stack of thick, fluffy towels. I take them from her and smile. I met Mara, the young hotel owner, when I arrived yesterday. She had kind eyes and a warm smile, and this woman seems no different.

"Thanks," I respond, turning to put the towels down next to my purse on the desk. I turn around and see the young woman turning to leave. "Wait!"

I rummage through my purse and find a couple dollar bills. I hand them to her and she frowns.

"What's this for?"

"It's a tip. For the towels."

She laughs. "You city people are so funny sometimes," she says, grinning at me. "Don't worry about the dollar. You're here for, what, a couple months? You really going to give me a dollar every time I knock on your door?"

"I hadn't really thought that far," I admit, staring at the crumpled bills in my hand. I hope I haven't offended her.

She shakes her head. "You had dinner yet? I was just about to head down to Harold's. You can use that money to buy me a drink. I'm guessing you don't know anyone in town yet."

"No," I say. "I don't." *Well, except for a certain Mr. Ethan Clarke, who I know a bit better than I should.*

Her eyes flash and a smile appears on her lips. "Well, I can introduce you to the main troublemakers," she says, grinning. "None of them bite, unless you want them to."

I'm about to refuse, to say that I'll eat in my room, but something stops me. It might be nice to spend an evening away from my thoughts. I might actually make a friend while I'm here. I nod. "Deal," I say.

"Good. I'm Katie, by the way," she says, extending her hand.

"Zoe," I reply as we shake hands. I like her smile, and I can't help but grin back.

"Heard you were in town to investigate the fire," she says, narrowing her eyes ever so slightly. Her question feels a bit too probing, so I try to skirt it.

"Not really. I'm working with the National Parks to minimize the risk of wildfires. I developed a set of procedures back in Seattle and they sent me here. The fire at the hotel construction site was a major incident, so I'm trying to work with the Rangers to help prevent it from happening again."

Katie laughs, and I'm not sure why. She throws her head back and lets out a full-bellied laugh, finally shaking her head. "Don't think it'll happen again. You can be sure about that."

"How do you know?"

Her eyes glimmer again, and she tucks a stray strand of dark hair behind her ear. "Wouldn't be any reason to!" I'm about to ask her more, but she nods down the hallway. "Come on, get ready and meet me in the lobby in ten minutes. I'll tell you everything you need to know."

She winks at me and turns down the hallway. I stare after her for a few moments before closing the door. This job doesn't seem as straightforward as I first thought.

I GET READY SLOWLY, frowning as I mull over her words. The Rangers said the same thing in the staff meeting–that there was little chance of it happening again. How can everyone be so sure?

Unless they know who did it, and why it was done. Katie said there wouldn't be any reason to start the fire again. Between that and Ethan saying it was started to stop the developers from digging up the forest, maybe the fire was started with somewhat noble intentions.

I step outside. The door to my hotel room closes behind me and I take a deep breath, heading down the long hallway toward the front of the building.

Katie is waiting for me, dressed in jeans and a t-shirt. She smiles when I appear in the lobby and nods her head toward the door.

"Come on," she says. "Harold's has the best burgers in town."

"Good," I answer with a grin. "I'm starving."

We walk in silence as dusk falls over the town. The sun has disappeared behind the mountains, sending brilliant reds and pinks across the sky. I inhale, staring at the vast landscape.

"It's so beautiful around here," I breathe. Katie smiles, inhaling deeply through her nose.

"I love the smell of the air here. I spent some time in New York City when I thought I wanted to leave this town, and the smells used to make me retch. Literally! Coming back home was the best thing I ever did."

"Don't go to Seattle, then," I laugh. "The smog in the city will choke you to death."

Katie makes a noise and we walk on in silence.

"So what were you doing in New York?" I ask after a pause.

Katie inhales deeply and sighs before answering. "I was restless, I guess," she finally says. She glances up at the peaks in front of us and shakes her head. "Then I clicked my heels together and said, 'there's no place like home'," she grins. "This town has a way of getting under your skin."

"I can see that," I say, glancing at the sunset again. My heart flutters and I take a deep breath. Audrey would love it here. My thoughts flick back to my conversation with her this morning, and worry snakes into my heart. I hope she's okay. I hope the kids at school aren't bothering her.

I watch as Katie kicks a pebble off the sidewalk, and I try to think of something to say. The seconds tick by in silence as we walk toward the other end of town, and after a little while it feels like I've waited too long to respond.

Finally, the curiosity that's been gnawing at me becomes too much to bear. With a deep breath, I change the subject and ask the question that's been on my mind since she dropped off those towels at my door.

"So what happened with the fire?"

Katie glances over at me and laughs. Her eyes spark again as she nudges me with her elbow. "Zoe, you have no idea what you've just stepped into. This is a multi-generational feud. Love, drama, cheating, crime, fraud, arson. It's got it all. Even an arranged marriage!" She sweeps her arm as she speaks, across the vista of mountains and forest and sunset sky in front of us. "And it all starts with a family called the Clarkes, who lived up on that mountain over there." Katie points to the tallest mountain in view, over to the left. The very top of it is flat, but it has a sheer cliff face that seems to fall for hundreds of feet, crashing into the forest below.

My heart skips a beat and I frown. *The Clarkes? As in... Ethan Clarke?*

I try to smile at the same time and feel my face contort into a weird expression. I just don't know how to react right now. Katie laughs again and I can't help but relax a little. I shake my head and smile at her.

"You've met Ethan Clarke already, I would guess. He's a Park Ranger."

I nod, trying to keep my face steady. "Yeah, we'll be working together."

"He has two brothers, Aiden and Dominic. Dominic is married to Mara, who you've met. They own the hotel."

I nod. "Right."

She starts firing names and families and places at me, and I try to keep up. Her laugh is easy, and as we get to Harold's she hooks her arm into mine. I feel myself relax, and I smile at her. It's nice to meet someone friendly.

I mean, Ethan is friendly, but it's nice to talk to someone that I haven't slept with.

"Don't worry, Zoe," she says with a laugh. "The Clarke Brothers look a lot scarier than they are. If you're not careful, you'll fall in love with one of them."

I stiffen and Zoe laughs again. "You and every other woman in town," she continues, mercifully ignoring the very obvious tension in my body. She points to a building up ahead.

"There's Harold's," she says. "Buy me that drink and I'll tell you a story."

12

ETHAN

I PULL up outside Aiden's garage, noticing Dominic's car parked outside. Both my brothers must be here. The lights are on, so they must be working on a car. I kill the engine and jump down, strolling over to the open door.

My brothers look up when I walk in.

"Hey, Ethan," Aiden says, glancing up briefly and wiping his hands on a rag. Dominic slides out from under the car they're working on and grunts a hello.

I nod to him. "Shouldn't you be at home with Mara?" I ask. "When's she due, anyway?" Dominic scratches his head and heaves himself up. He wipes his hands down the front of his old paint-stained t-shirt and sighs.

"Needed an evening away from it all. I think I was getting grumpy, because Mara pretty much ordered me to come here. She said the baby isn't coming out any quicker and my fussing was only annoying her."

I chuckle. "Sounds like Mara."

Dominic grins at me and nods to the fridge, tucked away in the corner of the garage. I head over to it and grab three cans of beer. My brothers nod as I hand them the drinks, and I nod back.

Sometimes, we spend hours without speaking a word to each other. My older brother isn't much of a talker, and all three of us brothers have developed a sort of non-verbal language to communicate. I lean against the work bench and crack open the cold can of beer.

"As long as this baby holds off long enough for them to clear the rockslide off the freeway, I'll be happy." Dominic stares off through the doorway at the sliver of horizon we can see through it. "The highway crew told me it would be another forty-eight hours before they'd get it cleared."

"You drove down again today?" Aiden asks, wiping his lips after taking a sip.

Dominic grunts. "Baby's due any day now."

The nearest hospital is about thirty miles away, to the north, and access to it is completely blocked by the rockslide. I chew my lip.

"There's no doctor closer?"

Dominic sighs, shaking his head. "They won't airlift her to the hospital in Albany for the birth unless it it's life-threatening. There's a midwife a couple towns over, but I'd just be a lot more comfortable if we could go to our regular doctor."

"How long does labor last, anyway? Doesn't it usually take hours? Could you drive to Albany?"

Dominic grunts again. "Doc said it would be best not to. Said the drive is too long and it wouldn't be safe."

He's still staring off in the distance and I take a deep breath. He's got a lot on his plate right now. Dominic crumples his can in his hand and tosses it in the trash.

"So what's up?" Aiden asks. I frown, and the two of them chuckle. "The last time you came here at this hour on a work night was to convince me to burn down that hotel."

I tip the can of beer back and savor the last few drops before tossing it on top of Dominic's can in the garbage. My brothers are still staring at me expectantly, and I shrug. The truth is, I don't know why I'm here. After spending all day trying to ignore the aching in my stomach whenever Zoe was near, I just wanted to get away.

Dominic and Aiden exchange a glance. Dominic grins at me. "I got to warn you, Ethan, my criminal days are over. I've got a baby girl to take care of now." His eyes are glimmering and I finally chuckle and shake my head.

"I'm not going to ask you to do anything illegal," I say.

"But...?"

"There's this girl," I start.

Aiden starts laughing, and a sharp flash of anger rushes through me. He shakes his head and looks at Dominic. Aiden's looking at me, shoulder moving up and down as he laughs until he shakes his head and grabs another beer from the fridge. He hands one to me and one to Dominic before cracking one for himself.

"It's always a girl," he explains. "Who is she? Is it Katie?"

"What? No! Why does everyone keep saying that?"

"She's been in love with you since you were nine, Ethan." He says as he tips the beer back. I look at the full can of beer in my hand and do the same before guzzling half of it down.

"It's not Katie," I finally say after wiping my mouth on my sleeve. "It's a woman I work with. She's investigating the fire."

Dominic's eyes narrow as his eyebrows come together ever so slightly. His chin dips down and I know that means *'keep talking'*.

"Well, she's not really investigating the fire. She works for the Parks, and she's consulting on how to improve our fire safety measures to prevent it from happening again. Or something."

"Right," Dominic says. Aiden stares at me for a while, and I know both of them are worried. Even though Aiden had nothing to do with the fire, most of the town thinks he does. And Dominic and I *definitely* had something to do with the fire.

We say nothing to each other for a while. Finally, Dominic looks at me.

"So is she going to cause trouble?" he asks.

I shrug. "I don't know. She could. She's nice, though!" Dominic sips his beer and stares at me. His eyes feel like laser beams and I try my best to ignore him. "I mean, I like her. As a person. Coworker." I clear my throat and avoid their stares.

"Stay away from her, Ethan," Dominic finally says. "If you get close to her, and she finds out you, me and the Sheriff burned that fucking building to the ground, you're going to get us all in serious trouble. I'm talking nationwide news. Can you imagine the headlines? *Police Sheriff accused of felony arson*," he says, sweeping his arms to highlight the words.

"You wouldn't even be the headline!" Aiden agrees. "Bill would take all the glory. And you'd drag me down along with you."

Dominic grunts in agreement. "Nah, you need to stay the fuck away from that woman. We've got families to take care of now."

"I don't want to go to jail either, guys," I sigh.

I take a deep breath, closing my eyes. All I see is Zoe. I want to tell them how amazing she is. I want to tell him about our weekend together, and the way she makes my heart thump. I don't want them to look so suspicious. I know they'd laugh if I told him about her walking into the office right after we'd spent the night together.

Something is holding me back. Maybe it's the thought of him chastising me for getting close to her when I know now that she could put us in prison. Maybe I just want to keep that weekend between Zoe and me.

I sigh and nod, throwing my empty away.

"You're right," I say to Dominic. "I'll stay away from her."

Even as the words leave my mouth, I'm not sure how I'm going to do that. I *work* with her, for crying out loud. And when I'm not working, I'm thinking of her!

Maybe it'll pass and I won't be so infatuated with her. Maybe I should just pursue Katie. Everyone seems to think it's meant to be between us.

I grunt to my brothers, who grunt back. Aiden nods his chin toward me and I nod toward the door. Dominic sits back down on the mechanic's creeper and lies back, grabbing the edge of the car they were working on. He looks at me and nods before sliding under the car again.

When I get outside, I take a deep breath.

I know he's right. I know I need to forget that night with Zoe ever happened, and I need to keep my distance. It's not just me that could get in trouble. It's the Sheriff and Dominic, too. Aiden could even get in trouble even though he wasn't there.

No, I need to stay away from her.

I bounce down the rutted road toward Main Street, letting out one last sigh. When I turn onto the road, I lean back into my seat and resign myself to the fact that I'm not going to feel Zoe's skin against mine again. Not anytime soon, and probably not ever.

There's a weight on my chest that doesn't seem to be leaving. I drive slowly, heading back toward the center of town. When Harold's comes into view, I frown.

A couple people are running. They're running in the same direction I'm driving, over to the far end of town. I glance at the horizon, looking for a sign of what might be going on. I turn off the radio and press my foot down, leaning toward the steering wheel as I accelerate. It doesn't look like they're out for an evening jog.

When I get closer, I see who they are. Zoe is with Katie, running down the street toward the edge of town. I roll down the window and slow to their pace.

"What's going on?" I holler.

Zoe doesn't seem to hear me. She keeps running, and Katie turns toward me.

"Get your brother," she pants. "Mara is in labor."

13

───────

ZOE

MY HEART IS THUMPING as I run toward the edge of town. My head is spinning and I'm not sure if it's because of what Katie was telling me about the fire and the Clarke brothers, or the thought that Mara McCoy will be giving birth any minute. I've only met her once, last night when I arrived, and her belly was bulging with the unborn baby.

Katie says a few words to a car but I don't have the energy to look over. She reappears beside me and we jog alongside each other.

"I hope Mara is okay," Katie breathes. Her face is drawn, with deep lines across her forehead. She shakes her head and speeds up.

"Is there no hospital to take her to?"

"The freeway is still blocked," she says. "We'll have to help her out as much as possible until we can find her a doctor."

"Is there no other doctor nearby?"

Katie snorts. "I'm not sure you realize how isolated Lang Creek is," she says. "Look around you."

She's right. Once I left Long Lake, it was nothing but wilderness until I saw the sign for Lang Creek.

We turn off the main road and down the long lane that leads to Mara's house. We pass a building that looks like a workshop, and I follow Katie straight to the main house. We burst through the doors. Katie rushes into the bedroom and I follow.

"Got your text," she says as we step through.

I immediately feel like I'm overstepping. I hardly know these women at all, and somehow, I've been admitted into the most intimate of places. Mara McCoy looks up at me, her face crumpled in pain as she doubles over, clutching her belly with both hands.

She moans, and I can see her stomach shifting. It contracts and moves as she moans in pain, and my own hand flies to my stomach. I remember that feeling. I take a deep breath, stepping backward toward the doorway.

Katie rushes to Mara's side and grabs her arm, helping her back down onto the bed. Mara lies back, and I see the thin film of sweat all over her face and neck. I swallow, and Katie glances at me. I can see the whites of her eyes and can almost feel the fear emanating off her.

Mara's eyes are closed and her chest is rising and falling gently. The contraction is over, and she'll have a few minutes of rest before the next one.

I remember how that felt. I remember the fear, the terror of knowing what was about to come. All the jokes about 'pushing a watermelon out' suddenly became a lot more *real*. I barely remember the pain of the contractions. I was in a hospital when I gave birth, surrounded by nurses and doctors and loved ones, in a haze of pain and adrenaline and medication.

Katie's mouth opens and closes again, and I watch her squeeze Mara's hand.

Something shifts inside me, and I take a step forward.

"Is it your first?" I ask. Mara's eyes flutter open and she seems to see me for the first time. Her chin dips down ever so slightly and a lump forms in my throat. I nod.

"Katie, go get as many towels as you can find. Get a bucket with cold water and we'll keep her comfortable. Do you have your doctor's phone number?"

"I have the hospital's phone number," Mara says. Her voice is weak, and she waves her arm toward a desk in the corner. Katie jumps up and mumbles something to Mara before rushing out the door. I head over to the desk and flick through a few papers.

"The post-it note," she says weakly. I glance up at the wall and see a name and number scrawled on a faded post-it note.

"Doctor Bertrand?"

"Mm" she says, closing her eyes and bringing her hand to her forehead. I grab the number and sit beside her on the bed. She's rubbing her stomach back and forth, taking long breaths. I put my hand over her arm as I call the number and wait to be connected. When I explain the situation, I'm put on hold and I glance at Mara.

"I'm Zoe, by the way," I say. "We met this morning. I hope I'm not intruding."

Mara laughs, and then groans. "I don't give a shit right now. I just want to get this baby out of me."

"I know the feeling," I say, almost to myself.

"You have kids?"

"Just one," I say. My hand finds hers and she squeezes it. "It's worth it, in the end."

Mara chuckles again. "I fucking hope so," she says. She takes another long breath. The phone clicks and an old, gravelly voice comes on.

"Doctor Bertrand speaking."

"Hi, Doctor," I say, shifting my weight and standing up. "My name is Zoe Randall and I'm with Mara McCoy. She's started having contractions. They're—Mara, how far apart are they?"

"I don't know," Mara groans, glancing at the clock. "Fifteen minutes? Maybe more?"

"They're fifteen minutes apart," I say into the phone.

Doctor Bertrand makes a noise and then sighs. "She's a couple days early. Of course this would happen. I'll get in touch with the midwife down in Glens Falls. I have her on standby for this reason. How is the patient?"

I glance at Mara, who's turned onto her side, clutching her stomach. Her mouth is open and her face is contorted as she lays in bed.

"She's... I mean, she's about to give birth, so she's not great." Mara snorts and the corner of her mouth lifts up. "But she seems to be okay."

"Put her on."

I pass the phone over to Mara just as Katie reappears with a stack of towels and a small bucket of water. She motions to the bed with the stack of towels.

"What's going on?"

"Doctor's going to try to get a midwife over."

She nods. "Good. Hey," she turns to me after putting down the towels, and then glances over my shoulder at Mara. "Thanks. I kind of panicked when we got here."

I shake my head. "I haven't done anything. I just called the doctor." Katie's lips pinch together and she glances at Mara again, who's still groaning over the phone to her doctor.

"Still," she said. "It's nice to have someone else here."

I try to stretch my lips into a smile and turn back to Mara. She hangs up the phone and looks at us through hazy eyes. "He's going to get a midwife," she pants. "Be a couple hours before she's here."

Her sentences are short, spoken between labored breaths. I nod and soak one of the towels in the cool water to put on Mara's forehead. She sighs in contentment and starts to relax. I look at Katie, who readjusts the pillows and pats Mara's hand.

"It'll be okay," she says to Mara. "We're here."

The silence in the room is only broken by Mara's breaths. She breathes in deeply and forces the air out of her nostrils. I can see the pain etched on her face, and I try to keep her as cool as possible.

We have a few minutes of peace until the door flies open and the largest man I've ever seen barrels through. I jump up, eyes wide and heart thumping as he rushes toward the bed.

"Mara!" he says with a hoarse voice. "Are you okay? The fucking freeway is still blocked! Fuck!"

Mara's eyes open and she grimaces at the man. "Zoe called the doctor and got the midwife to come. It's okay."

The man seems to notice me for the first time. He stands up, and even on the opposite side of the bed he seems to tower over me. He's got the same piercing blue eyes as Ethan, but he's taller and wider than the Clarke brother I know. This must be Dominic, Mara's husband. I nod to him, and he looks at me almost suspiciously. It's not until someone clears their throat behind him that I notice Ethan is here too.

"Zoe, this is my brother Dominic. Dominic, this is Zoe Randall. She's the consultant I was telling you about."

He was talking about me?

"I want her to stay," Mara says. She's staring at her husband fiercely, and he tenses. Dominic's eyes narrow, and he looks me up and down. Finally, the tension in the room dissolves and he grunts. I'm guessing it roughly translates to 'okay, fine', because Mara lays back in bed.

Dominic sits down beside Mara, and the bed dips under his weight. He strokes her cheek more gently than I would expect from a man his size, and leans over to kiss her forehead. My chest squeezes and he finally looks at me again.

"Thank you, Zoe."

"I haven't done anything," I say, waving my hand. "But we do need to get to work."

14

———

ETHAN

I WATCH Zoe out of the corner of my eye. She's stroking Mara's back as Mara leans over with her hands on the desk. She's breathing heavily and watching the clock anxiously as we all wait for the midwife. Doctor Bertrand called back with instructions, and Zoe has been the *de facto* leader of our little birth room.

Every time Dominic comes in, his eyes narrow and his back stiffens. He goes over to Mara and strokes her back, squeezes her hand, generally just emanating anxiety.

As Mara gets more frustrated with his stifling attention, Zoe will give him another task to do. She sends him to get some water, and then to the kitchen to get some orange juice. She sends him off to make sure the baby's bassinet and linens are prepared, and sends him off to get something to eat for us all.

When he comes back with peanut butter sandwiches, she looks at the plate of food and nods.

"That was quick," she says. "Thank you, Dominic." And then she sends him to chop some wood.

He glances at Mara, and then nods his head. I can see the relief in his eyes when he walks out of the room. Zoe keeps her head down and prepares all the towels and buckets and bits and pieces that the doctor told her to. She gets basins of water ready, and prepares plastic bags for garbage.

Most of all, she takes care of Mara. She squeezes her hand and puts a cold towel on her head. Katie is gone with Dominic to chop some wood that none of us need chopped, so it's just the three of us.

"How old is yours?" Mara asks with her eyes closed. Zoe glances at me before responding.

"She's seven. Turning eight in two and a half months."

"So you're past the baby stage," Mara breathes.

Zoe chuckles. "Way past it, yeah. She'll be a teenager before I know it."

Mara smiles, and Zoe puts a fresh towel on her forehead. I sit in a chair, feeling generally useless. I almost feel like I'm intruding.

I clear my throat.

"I didn't know you had a daughter," I say, looking at Zoe. She holds my gaze for a few moments and then nods.

"You never asked," she replies simply.

A pang passes through my chest. Even when we were entwined in bed, talking and fucking until three in the morning, she never mentioned her family. My eyes widen as another thought crosses my mind.

As if she can tell what I'm thinking, she answers my unsaid question. "Her father died when she was two," she says. "It's been just me and Audrey ever since then. She's with my mom now, until I get back to Seattle."

"I'm sorry to hear that," Mara says. I grunt in agreement.

I glance at Mara. She's lying back, with one hand on her stomach and the other clasped between both of Zoe's. The intimacy between them makes them look like they've known each other their whole lives. Maybe that's what motherhood does to women. It gives them automatic admission to an exclusive club, where they understand each other on a level that I never will.

I jump when the door opens, and a short woman in her late thirties comes in. She has a bit of a waddle, and grunts as she heaves a big bag of medical supplies onto the table near the door.

"Well, what do we have here!" She exclaims. She looks at me. "Father?"

"No, my brother is. He's just outside."

"Hmph," she says, opening her bag. "The wood chopper, I'm assuming." I stand up and get out of her way. Zoe glances at me and shrugs. "My name is Lulu. Doctor Bertrand told me about your situation, Mara, and I came as fast as I could. Now, let's have a look, shall we?"

She glances at me and Zoe and I clear my throat, wiping my hands down the front of my pants. "I'll give you some privacy."

Dominic and Katie reappear, and Zoe and I use the distraction to slip out the door. When it closes behind us, she lets out a big sigh.

"I'm glad she got here when she did. I was running out of things to give your brother to do."

I laugh. "I thought that's what you were doing."

Zoe laughs as we walk toward the front door. "He was just stressing Mara out. I can tell he loves her, but it was getting to be too much for her."

"Mm," I respond. We step outside and Zoe gestures to a path in the trees.

"You want to go for a walk? I feel like I need some fresh air."

I nod, and as soon as we take a few steps, both of us let out a sigh. "The air tastes so good here," Zoe says, staring up at the starry sky. "I didn't even know it was possible."

"It's a pretty special place," I say, glancing over at her. Her eyes are almost misty, taking in the vast expanse of stars above us. We walk in silence for a while, and I resist the urge to take her hand in mine. Every few steps, her shoulder brushes against mine and it sends a tiny thrill through my chest.

Finally, I ask her the same question again. "Why didn't you tell me about your daughter? We talked about so many things on Saturday night." *And it seems strange not to mention her.*

Zoe looks over at me and her face relaxes. She smiles at me, but her eyes are distant. "It seemed really personal. You were just a guy I met at a bar. It didn't seem appropriate to talk to you about my daughter. And then I found out I work with you, and I just had no idea how to react."

She nudges my shoulder with hers. "And like I said, you never asked."

Her lips curl up into a smile and she starts chuckling. She shakes her head and looks at me again, her grin widening.

"What are the chances, hey?"

I grin. "Started the job off with a bang, you could say."

Zoe laughs, and leans her shoulder into me. I move my arm behind her, brushing the small of her back. The path winds through the trees, and the sound of running water gets louder as we wander toward the river. Zoe stops and watches the running water. I look at the river for a moment, and then over at her.

"That's Lang Creek," I explain. "What the town was named after."

Her eyebrows raise a bit. "Looks like more of a river than a creek to me," she says.

I chuckle and make a noise to agree. The moonlight is making her skin look almost silver. Her eyes look dark, and her hair is tied in a high ponytail. A few rebellious strands of hair have found their way out of the hair tie and are blowing gently in the breeze.

Zoe looks at me, and her face is serious. "I can't get involved with you, Ethan."

I'm taken aback, but I nod. "I'm not asking you to."

"I know. But I also know that we get along, and I'm attracted to you. I'm just letting you know that I have a family back home, and we work together. It's just too messy. I'm not here for very long, and..." She trails off, glancing at the river's rushing water.

"I agree."

She turns toward me and looks at my face. She stares at me intently, and my chest starts to beat a little bit harder. Her words are still ringing in my ears, and I know she's right. Her tongue darts out to moisten her lips and my cock throbs.

Her eyes drop to my lips and she takes a deep breath.

"What?" I whisper as she shudders.

She lifts her eyes up to mine and chuckles softly, shaking her head. "I just really want to kiss you right now."

ZOE

I DON'T KNOW if it's the fresh air, or the stress of being with Mara and Dominic, or just my own insatiable desire for Ethan Clarke, but I can't help it.

The words slip out of my mouth and Ethan's eyes widen. His lips part ever so slightly and it only makes me want him more. The silence hangs between us, disturbed only by the sound of the river flowing by us and the leaves rustling in the night.

I can't read Ethan's face in the darkness. My heart grows in my chest and my cheeks start to burn as we stand there, frozen in silence. I'm not sure how much time goes by. It's probably just a couple seconds, but it feels like an eternity. Regret starts to creep into the edges of my mind, and I wish I hadn't said anything.

It's a dangerous game, saying those types of things. I work with him, and I have a daughter back home, and if what Katie says is true, he's at the heart of why I'm here. Ethan Clarke holds the key to finding out what happened at the hotel, and making sure it doesn't happen again. If what Katie told me is true, he's the one who lit the match that set the building on fire.

But right now, none of that seems to matter. The breeze carries the faintest smell of his cologne, mixed with the intoxicating musk of man. My mind whirls and takes me back to our first night together, when his smell filled my nostrils and my body was his.

Then, like a dam breaking, the tension between us cracks. Ethan takes a step toward me and wraps his arm around my waist. His other hand sweeps up along my jawline to the nape of my neck and I melt into his arms.

When his lips crush against mine, nothing else matters. Not the hotel, not work, not the woman giving birth in the house down the path. Nothing.

All that matters is this man in my arms, pressing his body against mine and taking me to a place I didn't know existed. He kisses me fiercely, tangling his fingers into my hair and pulling me closer to him. He deepens his kiss and I tremble, gripping onto his shirt and melting into his chest until I'm dizzy. The only thing holding me up is Ethan's arm around my waist.

We fall apart. My hand flies to my forehead and I stand a foot away from him, panting. I drag my eyes back up toward him and see his chest rising and falling just as mine is. His eyes are dark with desire as a blush stains my cheeks.

"Well, so much for not getting involved with each other," I say, staring at his swollen lips and wishing I could taste them again.

Ethan chuckles and takes a step toward me, running his finger along my cheek and tucking a strand of hair behind my ear.

"You're gorgeous," he breathes. His eyes are shining in the moonlight and he takes a deep, raking breath. I wrap my arms around his neck and we stand in each other's arms without speaking.

I chew my lip for a moment and stare at his face. The corner of his lip curls up.

"Why are you looking at me like that?" he asks. His hands are on the small of my back, and they drift down toward my ass.

"Did you burn down that hotel?" I blurt. My heart is thumping, and I study Ethan's face as my cheeks start to burn. Ever since Katie told me the rumors, my mind has been whirling. If it wasn't for Mara going into labor, I would have asked her a thousand questions.

Ethan's hands stop and he stiffens ever so slightly.

"What?" He says slowly, barely above a whisper.

"I've just... Did you?" My voice almost breaks on the last word. I so badly want him to say no. I desperately want the rumors to be just that — rumors. Ethan stares at me for a few moments, his eyes dark and his face completely still. Finally, his face breaks and he chuckles, shaking his head.

"You shouldn't listen to Katie so much, Zoe," he says. "She'll tell you everything except the truth."

"So you had nothing to do with it?"

"No. I did not burn down that hotel," he says. He shakes his head again and kisses the tip of my nose. I relax, and a smile floats over my lips.

"Sorry," I shake my head. "I just–"

"Shh," he says, laying his lips softly against mine. He squeezes his hands over my bottom and desire floods between my legs. I grab the collar of his shirt and kiss him harder, feeling his heartbeat against mine as the memories of our night together flood my mind.

He pulls away from me, glancing down the path as he takes my hand. "Come on," he says, and I follow him without a word. He leads me through the trees to a small clearing before turning back toward me and running his hands up under my shirt. I shiver at his touch, letting out a soft moan as his fingers send sparks flying off my skin.

My eyes are low as I look at him again, panting. My hands drop to my jeans, and I start unbuttoning them. His eyes brows rise up and his lips part.

"What are you doing to me, Ethan," I breathe. "You're making me crazy."

He runs his hands down over my hips, helping me pull my jeans down to mid-thigh. He groans, running his fingers under the waistband of my underwear. "So are you," he says, before he turns me around and wraps his arms around me. One arm covers my chest, letting his hand rest over my breast as he nuzzles my neck. His other hand dips down under my panties. When he feels the wetness of my desire for him, he groans. I put my hands up to brace myself against the nearest tree, pushing myself back against him.

I'm shaking with excitement, biting my lip and glancing back at him until I feel him pull my underwear down to meet my jeans. He trails his fingers through my slit and groans again, and I close my eyes, exhaling. I hear the crinkling package of a condom and I hold my breath until I feel him enter me, and I'm in ecstasy.

"Come on, we should get back," I say, as Ethan kisses me gently. We're dressed again, and I pat my hair to make sure it's mostly presentable.

He sighs, and nods. "We probably should, yeah," he agrees. He hooks his fingers into mine and leads me back down the beaten path toward Dominic's house. My body relaxes and I take a deep breath. My heartbeat starts to slow down again.

No, I did not burn down that hotel.

I hear his words over and over in my mind as we walk hand-in-hand back toward the town. As the lights of Dominic's house get closer, I drop his hand and he nods.

"Probably for the best."

"Probably," I say. "Wouldn't want Katie starting any more rumors."

I mean it as a joke, but Ethan just grimaces. The workshop and house come into view, and I peer at the light at the back of the house. I can't see anything through the curtains, but I know that behind them, Mara is either in immense pain or her body is flooded with joy and endorphins as she holds her new baby.

We walk in silence the rest of the way. The lights in the house seem unnecessarily bright, and as we make our way back to Mara's room, the noises from inside seem unnecessarily loud.

When we push the door open, I once again feel like I'm out of place, like I've been admitted to this inner sanctum where I have no business being. Mara's hair is matted to her head, and Dominic is sitting on the far edge of the bed with his back to us. Katie is busy tidying up with the midwife.

There are a million things to look at, but my eyes are immediately drawn to the tiny bundle in Mara's arms. Five impossibly tiny fingers are wrapped around Mara's index finger, and a serene glow envelops the couple.

I step to the side with Ethan, exchanging a glance with him. I smile, feeling my heart glow for Mara, Dominic, and their new child. I make to leave, but Mara lifts her head up.

"Zoe," she says, as if noticing me for the first time. "Would you like to meet the newest member of the McCoy family? This is Hailey."

I glance at Ethan again and take a step forward. My eyes start to mist up and a smile stretches across my face.

"Oh, Mara," I breathe. "She's beautiful."

"My little potato," Mara says, laughing and stroking the newborn's scrunched-up face. She glances up at me, her eyes shining. "Thank you for everything."

I shake my head. "I didn't do anything," I answer. It's the truth. All I did was call the doctor and made sure no one panicked. And then I disappeared into the forest with Ethan. I blush.

Mara smiles at me. "It would have been a lot more tense in here without you." She glances at Dominic and chuckles, but he's too busy running his huge fingers gently over his daughter's cheeks.

I stay for a few minutes, but I can't shake the feeling of being out of place. I say goodbye to the family, and with one last glance at Ethan I leave them and make my way back to the hotel.

When I lie back in bed at the hotel, I stare at the ceiling and a torrent of emotions rages inside me. I'm not sure what to think about Ethan, or work, or the fire, or the baby. My hand rests on my stomach, and I think of the way it felt to have Ethan inside me. It felt too good to ignore. He's woken something up inside me that I can't ignore.

I turn to my phone and find a photo of my little Audrey, and my heart finally quiets down.

16

ETHAN

I've never seen Sandy's face light up as much as when I showed her a picture of my new niece.

"Hailey Jane Clarke," I say, as she thumbs through the photos. I glance at my boss's face and I think I see her eyes misting up. She straightens herself up, handing me my phone and clearing her throat.

"Beautiful," she says, turning away from me. I think I see her wipe her eyes but she turns back around and nods at me. "I'll have to go meet her and say hello to the new parents this week. I'm sure they're exhausted."

"Mara had a rough night, that's for sure," I say.

We both turn when the door to the building swings open. Zoe steps through, and my breath catches in my throat. She's wearing her uniform, same as yesterday, but something in the way she walks makes my heart thump. She's almost glowing. She looks to me right away and a smile creeps over her face before she catches herself. Looking away, she drops her things on the desk we cleared for her and starts chatting with our coworkers.

Sandy brushes past me. "So I hear you were quite the hero last night!" She says to Zoe with that misty look in her eyes again.

Zoe blushes and shakes her head. "Not really," she laughs. "All I did was call the doctor. The midwife did everything."

"Don't be modest, now," Sandy says. "Everyone's talking about how calm you were and how you handled Dominic for Mara."

"Everyone? The baby was only born about eight hours ago," she laughs.

"Welcome to Lang Creek," Bryan says with a grin. Zoe's eyes widen and she looks at me as a blush creeps over her cheeks. I try not to grin. Bryan glances at me and winks, and I'm not sure why. Did he see something between the two of us?

I watch Zoe sit down at her desk with her back to me and I do the same. My thoughts drift back to last night, with Zoe in the forest. My cock pulses in my pants at the thought of it. It was probably the hottest thing I've ever done in my life. She wanted me just as badly as I wanted her, and that felt almost as good as being inside her again.

But then I think of what I told her.

No, I did not burn down that hotel.

I close my eyes and lean back in my chair, rubbing my temples. I lied to her. Bold-faced, no-question-about-it, definitely lied.

I *did* burn down the hotel last year. So did Dominic, and Sheriff Whittaker. We did it for the benefit of the town and the people that live here, but that doesn't change the fact that we did it. Zoe didn't seem to understand *why* we did it when I showed her the site of the fire. She seemed so happy when I told her I hadn't done it — when I lied.

My chest burns and I take another deep breath.

I wonder what would happen if I came clean? If I just told her the truth?

Would she report me? Would she understand? Would she turn around and never speak to me again?

I glance over my shoulder and watch as she gets up and heads toward the kitchen. She steals a glance at me and smiles, and the shame inside me burns a bit hotter.

I know *why* I lied. I lied to keep my brother, the Sheriff, and myself safe. I lied because she's not from here, and so she could never understand.

I lied because I want to make love to her again. I want to lay next to her and run my hands all over her body. I want to feel my cock buried deep inside her and I want to make her scream. Not only that, but I want to wake up next to her and watch her rub the sleep from her eyes as she smiles. I want to make her breakfast and hear her laugh at the silly jokes I make.

I want all those things, and I know that if I told her about my involvement in the fire, all that would disappear in an instant.

So in reality, I didn't lie for my brother, or the town, of the Sheriff. I lied for myself. I lied to give myself a chance to be with her.

My thoughts are spinning, and my emotions are reaching something like anguish as I sit at my desk and mull over my lie. Then, my phone buzzes in my pocket.

Want to hang out tonight?

It's Zoe. I glance up and see her walking back toward her desk with a mug of coffee in hand. She glances at me and winks. Before I can stop myself, the corner of my lips curls up into a grin.

Definitely. 7pm?

I press send and lean back in my chair. My heart is thumping in my chest, and I'm not sure if it's the guilt of lying or the excitement of seeing her again.

I jump when Bryan appears at my desk. He nods his head toward Zoe.

"So what's going on there?" he says, grinning and wiggling his eyebrows.

"What? Nothing!" I say, a little too loud and a little too fast. I sit up in my chair, shuffling my papers and tucking a pen into my shirt pocket. "What do you mean?"

"Oh come on, Ethan, I saw the way she looked at you." He leans over and stares at Zoe a little harder. "Can't say I'm not jealous," he adds.

Anger flares up inside me, burning up through my chest and tightening around my throat. I can feel the tips of my ears burning as I clench my fists, willing myself to keep my mouth shut. Snapping at him for saying something relatively innocuous is not going to help the rumor mill. Instead, I shrug.

"She's alright."

Bryan looks at me as if I've suddenly grown another head. "Alright? Dude, she's smoking hot! I haven't seen a girl like that in Lang Creek since 2003!"

"Are you keeping a journal of all the hot chicks that pass through?" I ask, deflecting his attention away from me.

"Might as well be," he grins. "Well if you're not going for it, I might just try my luck."

The same anger flares up inside me, but this time I'm able to control it. I chuckle and nod my head toward Zoe.

"Go for it," I say. "Let me know how it goes." *Knock yourself out. I already know how it's going to go.*

Bryan laughs and claps me on the shoulder. "Relax, Clarke," he laughs. "I told you, I saw the way she looks at you." I watch him walk toward Zoe's desk. He sits on the edge of it and smiles at me before leaning toward her.

"So, Ms. Randall, has anyone shown you the Lang Mountain Lookout? I'm heading that way now, if you're free you can jump in the truck with me."

Zoe smiles at him and I feel a jealous pang in my chest. "That sounds great!" She says, pushing her chair away from her desk. "I've been wanting to go up there. And call me Zoe," she adds.

"Sure, Zoe," Bryan says, getting up and staring at me with a shit-eating grin on his face. I roll my eyes but I watch both of them as they walk out the door. It's not until I hear the engine fire on that I turn back to my desk. My phone buzzes.

SEE you then xox

MY SHOULDERS RELAX and I smile. Bryan can take her to all the lookouts he wants, but I know that I'm the one she's meeting tonight.

17

ZOE

I TRY to focus on what Bryan tells me, but my mind keeps drifting to Ethan. I think he's giving me a history of the area, or maybe of the townspeople. The truck revs and bounces up the slope of the mountain until the narrow trail levels off. Bryan stops the engine and grins at me.

"This is called Lover's Lookout."

He wiggles his eyebrows and I laugh, shaking my head. "Don't make me regret coming up here."

Bryan laughs, opening his door. "Come on, you'll get a better view from up here."

I follow him down a short, narrow pathway until the trees suddenly stop and a rickety-looking, rusty handrail separates us from a long, steep fall. My chest immediately feels hollow and I stop well back from the handrail. Bryan turns back to me and grins.

"Come on, Randall," he says. "You afraid of heights?"

"I didn't think I was, but my heart feels like it just fell into my stomach. This is supposed to be romantic?"

I inch my way forward and peer over the edge, testing the handrail with two fingers. It doesn't move. I grab it with my hand and try to shake it, surprised to find it solidly anchored into the stone below. Bryan looks at me with an eyebrow raised.

"Satisfied?"

"For now," I laugh. He points to the mountains, naming them all for me. He points out the Ranger Station, the site of the fire, the McCoy hotel, and any other landmarks that I might know.

It's breathtaking. Lush, green forests crawl up the mountains. Scraggly, rocky peaks poke out the top of their green blankets, with clouds hugging the jagged peaks. The town of Lang Creek looks like a sleepy bunch of houses, with a river winding gently through the bottom of the valley where the town was built. Smoke curls from two or three chimneys.

The only mar on the landscape is the site of the fire. Even a year later, the charred remains of the construction site are clearly visible. My mind drifts back to my conversation with Katie, which was interrupted just as she started telling me about the Clarke brothers and the mess of rumors that surround their family.

I nod my chin to the fire site. "So why does everyone think the Clarke brothers did that?" I try to sound as casual as possible, and I think I succeed until I see Bryan tense. He might not be as forthcoming as Katie.

Bryan keeps his eyes on the charred mark across from us and shrugs. His voice is even when he speaks.

"There's always rumors about those boys," he says, waving his hand lazily. "When Dominic married Mara, it was the biggest thing since Brangelina."

I snort, wondering how long it takes for celebrity news to make it to this little town in the mountains.

"Why was it such a big deal?"

Bryan chuckles, almost to himself, and then whistles as he turns around, leaning on the rusty railing. My eyes widen and my heart does that jump again, and I try to step away from the railing. He sees my nervousness and chuckles, leaning a little bit more into the rail.

"Why don't you step away from the rail," I say, trying to hide the nervousness in my voice.

"What, this railing?" he asks, shaking it with his hand.

My heart leaps. "You're insane," I say.

My heart is racing as I watch him so close to the edge. Finally he shakes his head and pushes himself off, clapping me on the shoulder and laughing.

"You're alright, Randall. I wasn't sure about you at first, but I like you."

I roll my eyes. "Gee, thanks."

Bryan grins and I can't help but smile back. It almost feels like I've made a friend. He turns around and takes one last look at the view before heading back up the wooded path to our truck.

"The McCoys and the Clarkes had been feuding ever since Old Man Clarke died," he says, turning his head so I can hear him over his shoulder. "It would have been, oh, I guess about a decade ago."

I make a noise, trying to hide the intense curiosity that's erupted in my stomach. Bryan doesn't seem to notice. We get to the truck and he pauses, turning to me and lowering his voice as he leans against the vehicle.

"It all came to a head when the new hotel was being built. It came to light," he says, glancing around the forest as if there might be someone listening in this secluded corner of the mountains. "That the McCoys had part ownership of the new hotel. Well," he whistles. "That didn't sit right with *anyone*."

"So why does everyone assume the Clarkes did it?"

Bryan looks at me and frowns, as if he hadn't even considered the possibility that it *wasn't* the brothers.

"Who else would do it?" he laughs. "You've met Dominic, right?" I nod. He shrugs as if to say, *'there you go.'*

"Right, but was there any actual *evidence*? Seems to me like it fits nicely into this whole feud narrative."

Bryan grunts and heads over to the driver's side of the truck. We get in and he turns it on. Before putting the car in gear, he pauses. He looks over at me and seems to consider something.

"After the hotel burned down, Mara McCoy came back. She and Dominic shacked up, and Mrs. McCoy – Mara's mother – left town in a hurry."

I wait, because I don't know what to say. What does Mrs. McCoy leaving have anything to do with any of this?

"No one's heard from her. Left her husband, her businesses, her daughter. Everything." Bryan puts the car in gear and starts driving. He stares out the windscreen, his eyes narrowing as he navigates on the narrow, overgrown logging roads. "Now you tell me that it's not suspicious. If you ask me, she found out what her daughter's new boyfriend did, and couldn't face the idea of accepting him into her family."

"Mara and Dominic seemed happy when I saw them. Wouldn't that tear them apart if it were true?"

"Maybe," Bryan replies.

"Wouldn't it be more logical that Mrs. McCoy did it, and she ran away afterward? Did she get an insurance payout? She could be living it up in Mexico or something!"

"Maybe," Bryan repeats. He doesn't look over at me, and I chew my lip. There *has* to be some other explanation. Surely Ethan wouldn't be capable of *arson*?! And then for the two families to be united in marriage? It just doesn't make sense.

He *told* me he didn't do it.

Or maybe I just don't want it to make sense. I want to find something – anything – that will distance Ethan from this crime.

He told me he didn't do it, and I have to believe him. Every time I'm near him, my stomach does backflips and my heart starts thumping. The thought of him lying to me makes me want to roll down the window and throw up as we drive back toward the Ranger's office.

Bryan is quiet for most of the drive back, and I'm grateful for it. When we pull up to the station, he turns to me.

"So are you investigating this fire?"

"What? I... no. Not really. I'm mostly just auditing your safety procedures to make sure it doesn't happen again."

"You're not trying to find who did it?"

"I mean, that would help in the whole procedures. If I know how it happened, then we can work on having it not happen again."

"Do you want my advice?" His eyes soften, and his voice drops as he speaks. My throat starts to tighten and I no longer trust my voice, so I just nod.

"Don't ask too many questions. People think a certain way here, and you coming in here causing a commotion isn't going to change anything. Don't worry about the fire. Just write your reports and forget about the whole thing."

My heart is thumping, and I consider his words. He holds my gaze for a few more moments, and then his face lightens.

"But what do I know? I'm just an adrenaline junkie with an affinity for rusty old handrails," he laughs. "Come on, Sandy'll kill me if you're late for the meeting this afternoon."

I grin at him, but my mind is still spinning circles around me. When I go back inside, I glance at Ethan's desk and surprise myself when I feel a sense of relief at his empty chair. I need to think, and it's impossible to do that when his perfect body is anywhere near me.

18

ETHAN

Dusk is settling into night as I throw another pebble into the river. I'm here to meet Zoe and I'm a little early, but even the serenity of the forest and the flow of the river has failed to calm me down. My heart is thumping, and every sound makes me turn toward the path where Zoe will walk to meet me.

Finally, after an eternity, I hear light footsteps and her graceful figure comes into view. She raises a hand toward me and I step into the path. I open my arms and she gives me a hug, resting her head on my chest and sighing.

"Long day?" I ask.

"I think little Hailey's birth may have tired me out more than I thought," she replies, resting her chin against my chest and staring at me with her sparkling sapphire eyes.

"I hear you. I had to go do an extra round to the campsites this afternoon and then I was falling asleep at my desk. I have a feeling it wasn't Hailey's birth that tired me out, though."

"I'm taking you back to my place and I'm giving you the best orgasm of your life," I grunt. My cock is heavy and my whole body feels like it's on edge. It's like my skin is suddenly ten times as sensitive as usual, and every cell in my body is focused on Zoe.

"Ethan," she says, her voice muffled in my back. I pause, setting her down gently and running my hands up her sides until they rest on her waist. She runs her fingers up my arms and hooks her hands around my neck. I search her face and then touch my forehead to hers.

"Unless you'd rather go home?"

"The last thing I want to do right now is go home," she breathes. "But we work together, and..."

She stops talking when my lips cover hers, and I feel her melt into me. When I pull away, we're both panting. "We're not at work," I growl. "No one has to know."

Zoe grins. "I've only been here a couple days, but I can tell you that *everyone* will know."

I laugh, tucking a strand of hair behind her ear. My finger drifts down her cheek and I use it to tilt her head up toward me.

"You want to know a secret?"

She nods.

"I don't care what they say. I don't care that we work together. I don't care that you have a daughter and a life in Seattle. I don't care about any of that, because all I can think about is getting you back to my place and doing a thousand things to make you scream."

I tilt my head closer to her and brush my lips against the soft skin behind her ear. "I want to see that face again," I growl. "That face you make when you let go, and the orgasm ripples through your body."

She whimpers, and I lay a soft kiss on her neck. "I want to feel your legs shake and I want to hear you screaming my name."

Her hand tightens on my neck as her fingernails dig into me.

"You drive me wild, Zoe," I say, breathing in the smell of her. When I pull away, her eyes are shining and her lips are parted. Her chest heaves up and down as she looks at me with fire in her eyes.

Zoe drops her hand to my crotch, feeling my hard length through the thick denim of my jeans. I groan, watching her through half-closed eyes. She runs her hand back and forth, and finally shivers, hooking her fingers into my waistband.

"I want you so damn much, Ethan Clarke," she says with a husky voice that sends another shiver through my body. "Take me home."

19

ZOE

I DON'T KNOW what it is about him, but when I'm near Ethan I feel an almost magnetic pull toward him. After my talk with Bryan, I almost told Ethan that I needed the night to myself, but as my fingers hovered over my phone's keyboard, I couldn't type out the message.

Instead, I'm walking — well, jogging, scrambling, stumbling — hand-in-hand with Ethan back to his house. My heart is banging against my ribcage, and my veins are filled with fiery desire. There's an epicenter of heat in the pit of my stomach, and it urges me closer to Ethan.

He pauses when we get to his door, hooking his fingers around my neck and pulling me in for a passionate kiss. When we finally fall apart, my chest is heaving and it takes me a few moments to catch my breath. I watch Ethan fumble with his keys, and then move behind him and run my hands around his waist. I rest my cheek on his back and take a deep breath.

When he gets the door open, he twists in my arms and tilts my chin up with his fingers, laying a soft kiss on my lips.

"Welcome to my house."

"Thanks," I breathe as he takes my hand and guides me in. My eyes swing around the small room, taking in the comfortable furnishings and simple decor. It looks like a clean, log-cabin themed bachelor pad. There are thick curtains and rugs lining all available surfaces, and all the furniture looks handmade from local wood. I drop my purse on the floor next to the door as Ethan kicks his shoes off.

"There's beer in the fridge if you want one. I'm going to light the fire."

I wander over to the small kitchen at the back of the house, glancing through an open door to see Ethan's bedroom.

He makes his bed, I note as I glance inside. I find the beer and grab two, heading back to Ethan. He's blowing gently into the fireplace as a flame is flickering to life. Within minutes, the logs are crackling and Ethan sits back on his heels.

We watch the fire in silence for a few moments, and I watch him. The firelight flickers over his face, and a strand of dark hair falls across his forehead. He wraps his arms around his knees, and I watch the muscles of his arms and shoulders bunch and stretch as he moves.

I sit back on the sofa and smile as he turns toward me.

"Fire has always fascinated me," he says, sitting next to me. "On a basic level, it makes it possible for us to live and cook and socialize, but at the same time it's one of the most dangerous forces there is."

He puts his arm around my shoulders and takes the beer I offer him. We both stare into the fire and I consider his words.

"You know, I read that humans started evolving into what we are now when we started cooking our food. Our bodies didn't need so much energy to break down the food we were eating, so our brains were able to develop with all the extra energy."

"Is that right?" he muses, turning his head to look at me. He nuzzles his nose into my neck and I chuckle.

"Something like that. Don't quote me on it. You're tickling me," I laugh, pulling away from him. He takes my beer and sets it on the coffee table, crawling over me until he's resting on top of me. I hook my arms around his neck and smile. He touches his nose to mine and I feel a growl rumble through his chest. It sends a thrill down my spine and I inhale deeply, filling my lungs with his scent.

"How are you so sexy?" he asks, and I wonder if I'm supposed to answer.

"I work out," I grin.

"I'll work you out," he says, pushing his hips down onto me. I laugh, wrapping my legs around his waist and kissing his lips.

"I'm not sure you can handle me," I grin.

"We'll just have to see about that, won't we?"

Before I know what's happening, Ethan is lifting me up and marching me back to his bedroom. I laugh, wrapping my legs around his waist and hooking my arms around his neck.

"You really have a thing for picking me up today, don't you?"

"I just like having you in my arms," he replies, tossing me gently onto the bed as I yelp and giggle. He grins, climbing on top of me and laying his body on top of mine. The heat of his skin singes me, and he brushes his lips over my clavicle. He groans, laying soft kisses all along my shoulder and neck. I tangle my fingers into his hair and press my hips up toward him.

"You're so sexy," he groans, and I shiver. His fingers trail up my sides, under my shirt and his hands feel like fire. Then, it's like thunder clapping. The passion between us explodes. He pulls my blouse off over my head and I tear at his shirt. He bites the skin on my shoulder and grinds himself into me as I claw at his pants, kissing anything my mouth comes in contact with.

He rolls me over and I straddle him, sitting up for a moment to run my hands over his chest. He groans, leaning his head back and closing his eyes.

"Do you have any idea how good it feels when you touch me?" he growls as he runs his fingers up my thighs, wrapping his arms around my backside. Shivers run through my legs as his hands travel up to the small of my back.

"Some idea, yeah," I respond, closing my eyes as his touch sends me into a tailspin. He tilts his hips up toward me and I can feel the hard length of his shaft through our clothing. I look at him through half-closed eyes, biting my lip.

"This is such a bad idea," I say as I reach behind me to unclasp my bra. He groans as I pull it away and toss it beside the bed.

"Terrible idea," he agrees as his hands run up my sides to cup my breasts. He thumbs my nipples and another shiver passes through me.

"Worst idea I've ever had," I breathe as I unbutton his jeans and pull the zipper down. He lifts his hips to let me take his pants off and I sigh as I see the outline of the cock I've been dreaming of since the first night I spent with him.

"Destined to end in disaster," he replies as I stand up and unbutton my own jeans. He groans again as he watches me undress, and then reaches over to touch my panties. He runs his fingers between my legs and my knees go weak.

"Get on top of me," he commands, and I have no choice but to do what he says. My body takes me to him, and I shiver as his hands run up and down my thighs. I grind my hips on top of him and feel his shaft get harder in his underwear. He keeps his thumb near my bud, on top of my underwear so that every time I move, a shiver of desire passes through me.

The air between us is thick. My skin is scorched every time he touches it, and I feel like a coiled spring. He brushes his fingers over my bud, my ass, my stomach, my breasts, and every touch sends me reeling. I do the same to him, reveling in every groan and every grunt he makes.

Finally, the tension is too much. He grabs my waist and flips me onto my back, reaching over to his side table and pulling out a condom. I'm trembling with excitement as I watch him tear the crinkling package open and tear off his underwear. He slides the condom on and rips my panties down my legs.

My breath is shallow, and my body is ready. I gasp as he enters me, and the rest is a blur.

I've never made love like this. We're animals. We tear at each other, my nails leaving red scratch marks down his back as he drives his shaft inside me. My back arches and he nips at my neck, palms my breasts and thrusts deeper.

I'm gasping, moaning, bucking with him as we let the pleasure and desire take over. I'm on top of him now, and I yelp when he smacks my ass with his palm. It stings, and it sends a new wave of pleasure through me. I look over to the side and in a mirror, I see his red handprint on my ass. Something about the mark on my skin makes my blood turn to fire.

"Do it again," I breathe, digging my fingers into his shoulders.

"What?" he asks between breaths.

"Slap my ass," I pant. "Do it again."

His eyes flash and a grin tugs at his lips. "If you say so," he replies, and does what I ask.

That's the beginning of the end for me. In that moment, when I let myself open up and be carried away by our pleasure, I know I'm his. It doesn't matter what rumors surround him. It doesn't matter what rumors surround me, I'm his. We're linked. When my orgasm erupts through my body, his name is on my lips, his hands are on my body, and I'm his.

20

ETHAN

THE NEXT FEW weeks fly by. The days start to get shorter as summer rushes toward autumn, and my heart sings. Zoe and I steal any moment we can together. I think Sandy knows, but I'm not sure. Bryan grins at me whenever Zoe walks in, and I know the Lang Creek Rumor Mill is churning. We do our best to keep things quiet, but it's hard. Zoe is magnetic. It's almost impossible to hide.

At some point, we stop trying to hide it. People see us walking together in town, and the rumors fly, and then they stop. Katie and Mara meet us at Harold's some evenings, and my brothers meet Zoe and warm to her. Without me realizing how, we've slipped into a relationship that everyone seems to understand and accept without either of us having to really say anything.

I try not to think about the fact that Zoe will be leaving soon.

At work, Zoe briefs us on security measures and audits our procedures. She submits a report to Sandy after a few weeks with us, and I don't hear her talking about the hotel fire much after that. Sandy asks her to look at the other conservation programs we have in place. Zoe quickly adapts to life at the Park.

She's standing over Bryan's desk as they discuss an invasive beetle that seems to have found a home in the north-eastern part of our Park. I smile as I watch her laugh and talk with our coworkers. She's slipped into life in Lang Creek so easily.

Last night, we video called her daughter. She speaks to her every night, and I met Audrey for the first time almost two weeks ago. Since then, I've spoken to her a few times. She's precocious and funny, just like her mother.

Zoe stands up and stretches her back, glancing over at me and winking. Her phone rings, and she frowns before answering it. I crane my ears to try to hear who she's speaking to, but she ducks into the conference room. When she re-emerges, the smile is gone from her eyes and she looks troubled. A shadow is over her face and she slumps back into her chair.

I push my own chair back and head over to her desk.

"Everything alright?" I whisper, glancing around at the mostly-deserted office. Zoe lifts her eyes up to me as if she's noticing me for the first time.

"I, uh, yeah, actually," she says. "Everything is good. I just got offered a promotion. A really, really big promotion. The 'you-don't-turn-this-one-down' kind of promotion."

My heart sinks. "Oh," I say, trying to force a smile. "When do you leave?"

She shakes her head. "That's the thing," she says. "The promotion is here."

My eyes widen and my jaw drops. I'm not sure how to react. Zoe is staring at me, waiting for me to say something. I clear my throat.

"You don't seem too happy about it," I say as my chest tightens. A lump is forming in my throat as I watch the woman I've been seeing every day struggle with the idea of staying here.

She laughs mirthlessly, shaking her head. "If it were just me, I'd be jumping for joy. Being here is the best that's happened to me since Audrey was born. But that's the thing," she says, staring at me with pain in her eyes. "Audrey! Am I just supposed to uproot her whole life and bring her here, away from her friends and her grandmother and everything she knows?"

I lean against her desk and my heart slows down. *She wants to stay.* I have to keep the smile from my face as I consider the difficulty of her situation. I take a deep breath to try to quiet the thumping of my heart.

"Was that your boss on the phone? What did you tell him?"

"I said I'd think about it. I told him I had to think about Audrey."

I nod.

She puts her head in her hand and blows a big breath out of her nose. She inhales and looks at me. "I don't know what to do. I know *why* I want to stay here," she says quietly, staring at me. My heart jumps and I slide my hand over hers. She squeezes my fingers and shakes her head.

"But that just feels so selfish."

"Why don't you get your daughter over here? When does school start? A couple weeks from now? Fly her out and you can show her the town and the school, and see if she likes it. Then you can decide."

Zoe stares at me for a few moments. "I hadn't considered that. That's not a bad idea."

"Why not? If she likes it here, it'll be a lot easier to make your decision. Then you won't have to turn down your 'don't-turn-this-one-down' promotion." *And you'd stay here. With me.*

A smile breaks over Zoe's face and the shadow over her forehead disappears. She jumps up from her chair and throws her arms around me. I stiffen, not used to touching her in the office.

Zoe catches herself and pulls away, squeezing my shoulder as she drops her hands.

"I'm going to call my mom," she says. "I might be able to fly both of them out here by the end of the week. You could meet them," she says almost hesitantly, searching my face.

I smile. "I'd be honored." My heart thumps as I watch her duck into the conference room again, this time having a much more excited conversation. I rub my temple with my hand and take a deep breath.

Is this what I want?

I glance at Zoe and feel my heart pulling toward her. I haven't been this happy... I don't know, maybe *ever*. I *want* her to stay. But does that mean I want to be a dad? Would I be a dad? Would she expect me to take on that role? Would things between Zoe and I change?

Of course things would change. She'd have her daughter here, and we wouldn't be able to run off together whenever we get a moment. I watch her through the conference room window and am surprised that I don't mind the thought. Is it possible I might be excited about having Zoe and Audrey here with me?

The thoughts are flying around my head and I stalk out of the building, breathing a sigh of relief as I step outside. I walk over to a nearby trail and lean against a tree, closing my eyes and breathing deeply. When I open them again, Zoe is opening the door and scanning the parking lot for me. She sees me, and a smile splits on her face.

My heart lifts, and I feel excited and terrified all at once. As Zoe walks toward me, the breeze flutters through her hair and the sun makes her skin glow. She looks so incredibly beautiful that it almost hurts to look at her. She's like the sun, and I can't resist her pull. When she walks over to me, she throws her arms around my neck without a word. She kisses me, and the doubt in my heart disappears.

21

ZOE

WHEN I TELL my mother about the promotion, she makes a noise and is quiet for a few moments.

"I don't know what to do," I say. "They're basically creating a position for me here, doubling my pay, and offering me way better benefits. I'd be consulting for three National Parks!"

"That's very exciting, Zoe," she answers slowly. "Congratulations." I hear her shift the phone to her other ear and I take a deep breath.

"I was thinking you could bring Audrey out, so she could see Lang Creek. We have a couple weeks before school starts. If she's not willing to move here, then I can turn the promotion down."

My chest squeezes when I say the words, and my thoughts fly to Ethan. Turning the promotion down sends a needle of pain deep in my chest when I think about leaving Lang Creek and of leaving Ethan. But at the end of the day, Audrey needs to be the priority.

"Do you..." I trail off and take a deep breath. "Do you think it's a bad idea to bring her here?" A lump forms in my throat and it's hard for me to say the last couple words. My mother makes another noise and sighs.

"No," she says, "I don't think it's a bad idea. I think it's a wonderful idea to get Audrey away from the city and get her to experience something different. Knowing Audrey, she'll love it. And..."

"... And...?"

"Well, I'm not quite sure what went on at school, or who these girls are that she knows, but..."

Fear starts snaking around my heart and I stand up straighter. "Mom, just tell me," I say through clenched teeth.

"I think she might be bullied at school."

My stomach drops and I feel dizzy. "What? What do you mean?"

"She won't talk to me about it. Getting her to tell me anything that upsets her is like pulling teeth," she says. "No question who she got that from," she adds.

I ignore her quip. "Mom, how do you know? What kind of bullying? Is she okay?"

"It's those girls that she knows," my mom says. "I'm not entirely sure, but I found Audrey crying after school a couple times."

"What!"

"I didn't want you to worry! She's tough, Zoe, she's started to open up about it."

"Mom! How could you not tell me this? How did I not notice?" My heart start to break as my eyebrows draw together. My daughter!

"Listen, Zoe, all I'm saying is that going to see you, and maybe even moving somewhere new might be a good thing."

"… But…?" I prompt.

She's quiet for a few moments, and I stare out my hotel room window, chewing my bottom lip. I always feel like I need my mom's blessing, even though I'm a grown woman. If she's not happy with this idea, then it will break my heart to go through with it. My head is spinning. What if Audrey *is* being bullied? How could I have missed the signs? I *knew* there was something off about that friend of hers — what's her name? Megan! I could tell by the way Audrey talked about her.

My mom sighs again, and it feels like a hand is slowly squeezing my chest so that I can't breathe.

"But it'll break *my* heart to see you go, Zoe," she almost whispers. I hear her clear her throat and her voice betrays her emotion. "I'm being selfish, and I'm sorry."

"Mom, you don't need to apologize," I start, but she cuts me off.

"I should be happy for you. I should be celebrating. Instead, I'm sad that I won't have Tuesday night dinners with my girls anymore."

"Mom…"

She sniffles and clears her throat. "I'll tell Audrey when she gets home from soccer camp, and then you can call later and explain everything." Her voice is harsher, as if she's forcing herself to suppress her emotions.

"Mom…"

"I'll go over to your house to get anything that you might want her to bring. When were you thinking of flying her over?"

"Mom, stop!" I finally say. "First of all, I'm flying you both over. I'm not having my eight-year-old daughter come here on her own. And plus, I want to show you this place too! Who knows, maybe you'll want to move here with us!"

My mom pauses and sniffles and clears her throat again. "Alright, honey. I'll talk to you later when I have more control over myself." I can hear her voice relax ever so slightly. "Love ya."

"Love you too, Mom."

I hang up the phone and flop backward onto my bed. I hadn't even *thought* of my mom! I'd only thought of Audrey, but of course my mother would be sad we were leaving! She has no one else in Seattle. My heart squeezes. She might feel like *she* was being selfish, but now I feel like that too.

I close my eyes and put my hand over my forehead. I stay like that for many minutes, until I take a deep breath and force myself to get up. I glance out the window at the setting sun, and I try to shake off the heaviness in my heart.

I've been here for over two months, and the sunsets never cease to take my breath away. I watch the colors shift and change as the sun goes down, the dark mountains cutting jagged lines through the sky. I lean my head against the window frame, and I stare off into nothing as I try to quiet my whirling mind.

Ever since I got that phone call earlier today, I haven't been able to make sense of what's right. I *want* to take the promotion. I want Audrey to come here and I want to build a life with her, away from the memory of her father's death and away from the city. If she's being bullied at school, then I *definitely* want to get her out of there. I want her to experience something different, and I feel like I've found something special in Lang Creek. They've accepted me into their community so warmly, and I'd love for her to experience that before she's old and jaded.

And of course, I want to keep seeing Ethan. The look on his face when I told him about the promotion wasn't exactly jubilant, but when we kissed in the parking lot, his eyes had softened and his smile had been brilliant.

I jump when there's a knock on the door. I open it to see Katie, dressed in her regular clothes with her bag slung over her shoulder.

"Just finished work," she says. "You want to come to Harold's with me and Mara? There's a band on tonight. You might know the lead singer," she winks.

I open my mouth just as my stomach grumbles. Katie's eyebrows shoot up and she laughs. "Sounds like your stomach wants you to come!"

I smile and glance at the time. It's almost time to call Audrey. I nod to Katie, who smiles warmly. She, Mara, and I have become close over the past two months. Little Hailey reminds me so much of Audrey when she was born, and I think Mara has appreciated having us around to help out. Going out with them tonight will be a nice way to unwind after telling Audrey about the promotion and the possible move to Lang Creek.

"I just have one quick phone call to make and I'll be right over. Save me a seat?"

Katie smiles and nods. I close the door just as my phone starts to ring. My mom's face pops up on the screen and I take a deep breath, clicking to answer the incoming video call.

"Hey, monkey!" I say when my daughter's face appears on the screen. She smiles at me, and my heart softens.

"I'm not a monkey, Mom," she says, rolling her eyes like only eight-year-olds can.

I laugh. "You're my little monkey!"

"Grandma says you have some good news for me."

"I do. How would you feel about coming to visit me?"

Her eyes brighten and a smile breaks over her face. "Really?!"

"Really." Audrey jumps up and down excitedly and I laugh. Maybe this is the right thing to do.

I take a deep breath. "Audrey, when you get here, I want you to tell me if you like it here. I've gotten an opportunity to stay here, and I want to make sure you like it, too."

Audrey's smile fades a little and she frowns. "I would leave here?"

"Yeah, munchkin. We can see if you like the school and if you meet anyone that you'd like to be friends with."

Her face falls and a frown appears over her forehead. "A new school?"

My heart squeezes and I take a deep breath. "Audrey, are kids at your school ever mean to you?"

She looks away from the camera and down at the ground in front of her. A pain passes through my chest and I wait for her to speak. She shrugs. "Just Megan, sometimes. And then everyone laughs at what she says."

I take a moment before I speak again because I don't trust my voice. Anger flares in my stomach, and if that little Megan brat was in front of me, I'd want to wring her neck. I take a deep breath.

"How would you feel about meeting some new kids? If you don't like it here, you can tell me and we'll figure something out."

Audrey chews her lip, finally lifting her eyes back up toward the phone. "What about Grandma?" Her voice is getting higher with every question and my chest tightens. A lump forms in my throat and I try to swallow. I'm starting to regret this.

"Honey, don't worry. Let's just start with a visit and we'll see from there, okay? Grandma will come with you to visit. It'll be an adventure! You can climb a mountain and scream when we get to top!"

Audrey's eyes brighten and she laughs. "Really?"

"Really. I can't wait to see you, I've missed you."

"Me too, Mom."

I lie back in bed and before I know it, I've been speaking to Audrey for almost an hour. She eases the stress in my soul and soon I'm laughing with her as she tells me about soccer camp and piano and all the things that an eight-year-old finds to talk about. When we hang up, I sigh and clutch the phone to my chest.

I hope she likes it here. I have to put aside my feelings for this town and for Ethan and do what's best for my daughter. No matter what happens in my life or in my job, she has to be the priority.

22

───

ETHAN

"CALM DOWN, ZOE," I laugh. "You'll wear my carpet out if you keep pacing like that."

"What if Audrey doesn't like it here?"

"She's eight. She'll adapt."

"I know, but I don't want to rip her away from everything she knows. Her father died when she was young and that was trauma enough for one childhood."

"Come here," I say, opening my arms and wrapping them around her. "It'll be fine. It won't be traumatic for her. She'll get here tomorrow morning and she'll love it."

Zoe has been on edge ever since she got the phone call offering her the new position last week. She's so tense in my arms, and I try to rub my fingers through her hair to massage her scalp. She groans, and the tension in her body eases just a little.

"What will I tell her about you? What is going on between us?" Her voice is muffled in my chest, and she pulls away to look at my face. Her eyes are shining, and her eyebrows are drawn together.

"She's met me. She knows I exist."

She searches my face and I sigh. "I know. Do I say you're my boyfriend? My special friend? I haven't dated anyone since Mark died."

Her eyebrows raise in question and I sigh again. "I don't know, Zoe. I've never dated someone with a kid. I like you, Zoe." It's hard for me to say more, because a lump has mysteriously appeared in the middle of my throat. Zoe nods.

"I like you too. I feel like a bad mother."

"What! Why?"

"Because I've been here, shacking up with a sexy mountain god, and my daughter is back home by herself!"

"First of all," I start, touching the back of my hand to her cheek. "She's not by herself. She's with her grandmother, and from the sounds of it she's having a blast." Zoe scrunches her face and reluctantly nods. "And second of all," I continue as the corners of my mouth tug upwards. "Did you say sexy mountain god?"

"Don't let it go to your head," she says with her face stern but her eyes smiling.

"Sexy mountain god," I breathe, staring off out the window as Zoe smacks my chest and pulls away.

"This is serious!"

"So when you say sexy mountain god, is that just physical, or sexual, or...?" I glance at her and see her fighting to keep a smile off her face.

"I'm prone to exaggerating," she says, shrugging and glancing at her nails. "It's just an expression." Her mouth is starting to curl upwards and I stretch my arms behind my head.

"Right. Of course. I've just never heard that *particular* expression before. And it seemed to ring pretty true to me, so I was just trying to clarify what exactly–"

"Oh my gosh, Ethan, be quiet, please," she says, wrapping her arms around my neck and finally laughing. "You're the sexiest man I've ever seen. Physically, you're perfect. Sexually, you turn me on like no one before. Mentally, you're intriguing and captivating. Happy?"

She tilts her head to the side and raises an eyebrow. I press my palm in the small of her back and run my other hand over to the soft curve of her bottom.

I shrug. "Your words."

She laughs then, and her shoulders relax. I pull her closer and brush my lips against hers. She shivers and sighs.

"Thanks, Ethan," she whispers. "I'm just freaking out."

"Everything will be fine."

I dip my chin down again and lay a soft kiss on her lips. She curls her fingers into the nape of my neck and pulls me in for a deeper embrace. I hold her close, feeling every tremor that passes through her as if it were my own body.

The heat in my veins fires up, as it always does when I touch her, or look at her, or think about her. All I want to do is kiss every inch of her body and feel her skin against mine. I run my hand under her shirt and feel the heat of her skin again my palm, and another tremor passes through her.

She moans gently, and her kiss becomes more insistent.

I groan and pull her closer. I can't get enough of her. We've seen each other almost every day for the past two months, and somehow, I still miss her when she's not beside me. I inhale, filling my nostrils with her smell as my body tenses with desire. I kiss the soft patch of skin behind her ear and brush my lips down her neck.

Somehow her shirt evaporates, and so does mine. I press my chest against hers and wrap my fingers into her hair. My body is on edge, and my vision is zeroed in on only one thing: Zoe.

Just as my hand drops down to the fly of her pants, my front door bursts open. Zoe yelps. She jumps away from me and grabs the nearest thing to cover herself, which happens to be a cushion from the couch. Her eyes widen as she sees the hulking man in my doorway. A blush warms her cheeks and I turn to the intruder.

"Aiden," I say. "You heard of knocking?"

My eldest brother grunts, and I notice the darkness in his eyes.

"What's going on?"

"Hi, Aiden," she says, still clutching the pillow to her chest. I find her shirt and hand it to her. She hides behind me and shrugs it on.

"What's up?" I ask my brother, who has politely averted his eyes as Zoe gets dressed.

"Margaret McCoy is back," he says, and the blood drains from my face. *Margaret McCoy – Mara's mother. The woman who tried to buy this town by building the big hotel. The one who vowed revenge on my brothers and me for burning down the hotel.* I glance at Zoe, who's looking at me with her eyebrows drawn together.

"What do you mean, she's back?" I ask, glancing at Aiden again.

He shrugs. "Wanted to meet her granddaughter, I guess. Dominic is mad. You need to come."

My thoughts flash back to last year, when Dominic got so mad he decorated his front yard with shards of broken furniture. He smashed a chair so completely that we were finding splinters of it for weeks. So, if Dominic is mad, it's not good. I nod to my brother, whose face darkens as he turns and stalks out the door.

Zoe looks at me, wide-eyed.

"She's the one who disappeared after Dominic and Mara became an item?"

I nod, trying to ignore the hollowness in my chest and the dread creeping into my heart. Zoe chews her lip.

"Do you want me to wait here? I can go back to my room at the hotel when all this is blown over."

I shake my head. I want her beside me. Whatever Margaret McCoy wants, I'm sure there is some ulterior motive. She never cared about her daughter, so I doubt she cares about her granddaughter. Zoe is good at reading people, and it will help to have an outside opinion.

"I'd like you to come with me."

She swallows. After a pause, she nods without saying a word.

23

———

ZOE

MY HEART IS in my throat as Ethan parks the car in front of Dominic and Mara's house. He grabs my hand and we hurry to the front door together. I glance up at the windows, trying to glean some sense of what's going on inside. Most of the windows are dark, like black eyes staring out at us in the night.

"So why did Margaret McCoy leave again?" I ask, breathless, as we head toward the door.

"She tried to use Mara as a bargaining chip in one of her business deals by marrying her off the highest bidder. Dominic had to go all the way across the country to get her back."

My eyebrows shoot up, and I look at Ethan. His face is dark, and he squeezes my hand. We step into the lobby and I expect to hear shouting and fighting, or at least raised voices.

Instead, I hear nothing.

The whole house is silent. Ethan pauses long enough to glance around as his brows draw together. He slips his hand out of mine and a sense of dread starts seeping into my heart

I shouldn't have come. This is a family issue. Why am I here?

Ethan nods his head toward the front door, taking a deep breath. We stand on the front stoop and still, I can't hear anything. Ethan looks at me. I raise my eyebrows in question and he shrugs.

Raising a hand, he raps his knuckles lightly on the door.

"Come in," Mara's voice floats through.

Ethan wraps his fingers around the door handle and takes a deep breath before pushing it open. My heart is thumping, and I'm not even sure why. I brace myself for what I'll find on the other side of the door, peering around Ethan's body through the opening.

It's not what I was expecting.

Based on Aiden's tone before, and Ethan's reaction, I was expecting something... I don't know... morbid? Some sort of fight?

Instead, Margaret McCoy is sitting on a rocking chair with little Hailey in her arms, cooing gently at her granddaughter. Mara is tidying up the baby changing table. I look around for any sign of the older Clarke brothers, but they're nowhere to be found.

Mara sees me and smiles. Her face looks drawn, but there's nothing in her demeanor that would say that something is seriously wrong.

"Zoe! Come in. Hi, Ethan," she adds with a nod of the head. "You guys want some tea or coffee?"

"No thank you," Ethan says in a low voice. "I was actually looking for Dominic."

"He's at the workshop," she answers. I glance between Ethan, Mara, and Margaret, not understanding what is going on. There seem to be layers and layers of history between these people that I can't even begin to comprehend.

Mara's mother looks up from the baby and glances at Ethan. I see something flash across her face–a look of pure disgust mixed with anger–and a shiver passes down my spine. Her look is gone in an instant, and I'm left wondering if I imagined it.

It could be that I'm just taking what Ethan's told me about her and projecting it onto her. From where I'm standing, she looks like a doting grandmother.

"Ethan Clarke," she says slowly, looking him up and down. He freezes beside me, and I can sense the tension emanating from him.

"Margaret," he replies through clenched teeth. I'm afraid to breathe, afraid to move, afraid to do anything that might get in the way of this meeting. Mara glances at the two of them but avoids my eye.

"What are you doing here?" Ethan continues.

"I heard I had a new granddaughter. Can't a grandmother come visit her first and only grandchild?" She clutches the baby closer to her chest and I feel Ethan tremble beside me. The baby starts fussing in her arms and Margaret shakes her head. "Go find your brother," she says sharply. "You're upsetting the baby."

"*I'm* upsetting the baby?! I'm nowhere near the baby!" Ethan says a little too harshly, and Hailey starts crying. I put my hand on Ethan's arm. He looks to me, and I give him a loaded look. His shoulders slump and he stalks out the door.

I watch him leave, wondering if I should follow. Mara clears her throat and forces a smile.

"Uh–Zoe, this is my mother, Margaret." She gestures toward the older woman and I nod.

"Nice to meet you," I reply mechanically.

Margaret McCoy tilts her head to the side and stares at me through slitted eyes. An eerie smile floats over her lips and she nods. "Nice to meet you too, Zoe. How did you come to stay in our little town?"

"I'm here for work," I explain. I glance at Mara, trying in vain to read her expression. Surely she would be upset that the mother who abandoned her last year would suddenly reappear? Why would she welcome her into her house and let Margaret hold her newborn baby?

I clear my throat and nod to them. "I have an early morning tomorrow," I say by way of ending this awkward encounter. I feel oafish and out of place in the room, like I'm definitely intruding where I shouldn't be. Mara smiles at me kindly.

"I'll see you tomorrow, right? I have our dinner planned out already," she says. "I can't wait to meet your family."

I relax a bit and nod to my friend. "I'll see you tomorrow." I glance at Margaret, who is still staring at me. "Nice to meet you, Margaret."

"Likewise," she says, barely moving her lips. I duck out the door and breathe a sigh of relief. Across the lawn, the lights in Dominic's workshop are on. I cut across the grass toward it, hoping to find Ethan to tell him I'll walk back to the McCoy Hotel.

When I get closer, I can almost feel the tension sizzling in the air. The brothers are speaking in low voices, and I pause when I get close.

"When did she get here?" That's Ethan's voice. It sounds strained.

"This morning," comes a deep growl. Dominic, I think. It could be Aiden, but I'm not sure.

"Why is she back?"

"To cause trouble. Why else would she be back! All she ever does is look out for herself."

"Last time she was here, she was exposed for the cheating, manipulative woman that she is. She basically tried to sell Mara off to get married! I thought I'd never have to see her face again," Dominic says. I can hear the pain in his voice.

"Look," Ethan says, "try not to freak out. I don't want her here as much as the next person. The last year has actually been peaceful in this town. But I mean... maybe she *is* just here to see her granddaughter? If Dad was having an affair with her, she has to have *some* sort of redeeming quality, right?"

"I've never seen it," Dominic grumbles.

"It's *trouble*," the third voice says. It must be Aiden. "What about your new girlfriend? She was looking into the fire, and now with Margaret Fucking McCoy back in town I'm sure questions will start adding up."

The voices get lower and I crane my neck to try to hear them. Their voices are muffled, and I take a few steps forward.

The questions will start adding up?

What is that supposed to mean? I still can't make out what they're saying. They seem to have moved further into the workshop. I take one more step and the grass ends as my feet crunch on the gravel pathway leading to the workshop. My heart skips a beat as their voices pause, and the door to the workshop flies open.

Dominic's lumbering body fills the entire frame and I yelp, jumping back.

"I, uh, Dominic!" I exclaim. "I'm sorry! I was just inside, and I'm going home. Ethan... walking." My face is flushed and I can't meet his eye. I put a hand to my chest and finally force myself to make eye contact with him. He grunts, and steps aside as Ethan appears.

"I'll drive you home," he growls. His face is dark and his eyes are troubled.

I shake my head. "It's okay, really. I'd rather walk. Enjoy the last of the summer, you know?"

My heart is still thumping, and Ethan stares at me for a few moments. Not for the first time, I wonder who exactly he is, and what happened with the fire last year. Was he telling the truth when he told me he had nothing to do with it?

He nods his head slowly and steps toward me. With a deep breath, he rakes his hand through his hair and shakes his head.

"I'm sorry, Zoe. I shouldn't have brought you here. I thought you'd be able to tell me what you thought of Margaret, and maybe figure out what her intentions were."

"It's okay," I say. The words hang between us, and he stares into my eyes. He takes another step forward and brushes his hand over my cheek.

"You look beautiful in the moonlight," he says so only I can hear it.

My heart flutters and I smile for the first time since we left his place.

"I'll see you tomorrow. Can't wait to meet Audrey," he says, leaning down to lay a soft kiss on my lips. I nod, wrapping my arms around his waist and leaning my head against his chest. He puts his hand over my head and holds me for a few moments, and my whole body relaxes.

I have to believe him about the fire. If I don't, then I'll lose him.

We pull apart and he kisses me again, squeezing my hand. "Be careful," he says.

"See you tomorrow."

I walk away, forcing myself not to look back. My mind is troubled, and I don't know what to think. Regret starts to seep into the edges of my heart when I think about bringing my daughter across the country to come here. Do I really know these people? Do I really know what happened last year, with the fire or with Margaret McCoy or with any of it?

I take a deep breath and let the clean, cool mountain air fill my lungs. When I exhale, I feel more relaxed. Tomorrow, my daughter and my mom will be here. My mother will have fresh eyes on the situation and as usual, she'll be able to counsel me. Tomorrow, things will make more sense.

24

ETHAN

"YOU'RE GETTING TOO close to her," Aiden says to my back as I watch Zoe walk away. I turn around as anger flares up inside me, but I know he's right. "She's here because of the fire that you and Dominic and Bill Whittaker started. Remember, you and Dominic and the *Sheriff*? Felony arson?"

"I fucking remember, Aiden," I grumble. I glance back down the road to where Zoe disappeared and shake my head. "She's okay. She doesn't know anything."

"Yet," Dominic corrects. "She doesn't know anything yet."

He glances toward the house and I know he's thinking about the newest visitor in town: Margaret McCoy. If anyone will be able to sniff out my weakness for Zoe, it'll be her. And if anyone will want to exploit it, it'll be her, too.

AFTER A FITFUL SLEEP and a long day, I'm just about ready to head over to Dominic's house for dinner. He and Mara have invited Zoe and her family over for dinner. When I pull on a clean t-shirt, I take a deep breath and hesitate. Will Margaret be there?

If she is, I don't want to go. I grab my phone off the table, wanting to call Dominic and ask. My finger hovers over the 'call' button and I hesitate.

I think of Zoe yesterday, as she paced the floor of my living room. I think of the way she melted into my arms when I wrapped them around her, and how worried she's been about this promotion. My heart ached for her. Then, she came with me to Dominic's house without hesitation.

And now? Now I'm ready to let her down just because *that woman* is in town. I click my phone screen off and slip it in my pocket. If I want to be with Zoe, and I do want to be with her, I'm going to have to suck up my discomfort and face Margaret if she's there.

A thousand thoughts run through my head as I drive down Main Street toward the other end of town, where Dominic and Mara live. I glance in shop windows and at everyone walking by, trying to spot Margaret McCoy. If I see her somewhere else, it means she won't be at dinner. When I pass the last building and turn off onto the long gravel drive to Dominic's house, I shake my head.

Get a grip.

If she's there, I'll deal with it. Plus, there are no guarantees that she'll be at dinner at all!

I park my truck and jump out, scanning the cars that are parked outside. So far, I only see Dominic's pickup, Mara's car, and Zoe's rental. Things are looking positive so far, at least. I grab the pack of beer I brought from the passenger seat and head toward my brother's house.

The front door is unlocked, as usual. They live in a small, two-room house. It's more of a cabin, really. Dominic, Mara, Zoe, a little girl and an older woman are all crowded near the back of the room, in the kitchen. Aiden, Maddy and their two children are on the couch. Mara is pointing.

"We'll build the second bedroom over here, so Hailey can have her own space. We've got so much room to build out, it just makes sense to add on to this house."

"It's gorgeous here," the older woman says. She sees me in the doorway and smiles. Her eyes are kind, and they crinkle at the corners as she turns toward me.

"And this must be Ethan!" She exclaims with her arms outstretched. "Zoe, you never told me he was so handsome! The camera doesn't do you justice, Ethan.

A blush warms my cheeks and I glance at Zoe. Zoe grins.

Before I know what's happening, I'm being wrapped in a big hug. Zoe is laughing. "Ethan, this is my mother, Bernadette."

"Call me Bernie!" She says, holding me by the shoulders and looking into my eyes. She narrows her eyes and then nods, satisfied. "You got a good one, Zoe," she says with conviction.

I laugh. "You can tell that by just looking at me?"

Bernie taps the side of her nose and winks. "Mother's intuition."

Mara laughs. "I'm still waiting for mine to kick in," she says, glancing at the baby sleeping in her bassinet in the corner of the room.

"So am I," Zoe says, putting her arm around the little girl. She gestures toward me. "Audrey, this is Ethan."

Audrey stares at me for a moment. "Are you my mom's *boyfriend*?" She says the last word as if it leaves a sour taste in her mouth, scrunching her face and looking at me dubiously.

"Audrey!" Zoe says, her eyes widening. She looks at me and mouths the word *'Sorry!'*

I take a deep breath. I can relax. Yesterday was just a hiccup, and soon life will be back to normal. Mara takes Audrey by the hand and they start chopping something in the kitchen. Bernie grabs a bottle of wine from the counter and pours a few glasses, and we all slip into an easy conversation. Even Aiden looks relaxed, as if Margaret's arrival yesterday didn't worry him at all.

My chest feels warm as Zoe sits down beside me on the couch. She snuggles into my shoulder and I put my arm around her, kissing her temple and breathing in the smell of her skin. I close my eyes for a second and let the happiness of this moment sink in.

"So, Bernie," I say, turning to the older woman. "What do you think of our little town?"

"I think it would be the perfect place for a retiree like me," she says, winking at Zoe. "Zoe thinks she can just move away, but she won't get rid of me so easily!"

Zoe laughs, and shakes her head. "Mom, if you moved here with us, I would be over the moon. You know that."

"Well, that's settled, then," Bernie says with finality. "All three of us are moving here. You'll have to find me one of these sexy mountain men," she adds, waving to my brothers and me. "I like them a bit older, of course, but this general look is quite alright with me."

"Mom!" Zoe exclaims, laughing.

Mara joins in the laughter from the kitchen. "They're hard to resist," she says. "I tried to get away but I was dragged all the way back."

"Dragged!" Dominic exclaims, and everyone laughs again.

It's an easy evening. The past two months, Zoe and I have been stealing moments together, trying to ignore her inevitable departure from Lang Creek. This is the first time that we've been together with our families, and instead of feeling overwhelming, it feels incredibly *good*. I squeeze Zoe's shoulder and she leans into me. I glance over at Audrey, busy in the kitchen with Mara, and for the first time in a long, long time, I feel like I have a family again.

It's not until I'm driving home with a full belly and a full heart that I realize how lonely I've been. Ever since my parents died over a decade ago, my brothers and I have been floating out here, on our own. I've watched them find their wives and start families, and the gnawing envy inside me has grown.

Now, happiness actually seems possible for me.

As I pass the McCoy Hotel, I look up at the building. One of the lights in the top windows is on, and the curtain moves as I glance at it.

Margaret McCoy appears in the window. The hairs on the back of my neck stand up, and I squint my eyes up to see her more clearly.

I can't make out her face, but I know she's watching me. She stays at the window as I drive down the road until I turn my head forward and try to shake the uneasy feeling away.

The warmth in my heart is replaced with an ominous chill, and the smile fades from my face. I tighten my hands over my steering wheel and press my foot down on the pedal, watching the road in front of me until the McCoy Hotel is out of sight.

25

ZOE

"CAN I GET SOME CANDY, MOM?" Audrey asks, turning her head up to look at me with pleading eyes. "Please?"

I grin. "Fine. *One* piece. It'll rot your teeth."

Audrey smiles and disappears into the corner store. I wait outside with my mother, watching my daughter through the shop window. She walks slowly along the wall of candy, inspecting her choices. I turn to my mom and shake my head.

"She's got me wrapped around her little finger," I say with a smile.

My mother laughs. "Welcome to motherhood," she grins. "What do you think you were like when you were little?"

I grin and shake my head. "I wasn't that bad," I answer, nodding toward the shop.

"No," she agrees. "You were worse."

I laugh and nudge my mom, who puts her arm around my shoulder and kisses my cheek. "Am I still allowed to kiss you even though you're grown up?" she teases.

I just glance at her and grin.

Her eyes are sparkling and her skin looks brighter. Her cheeks are rosy, and I think she's standing up straighter. I watch her take a deep breath and exhale with her eyes closed. She groans and shakes her head.

"The air actually *tastes* good here," she says, opening her eyes and looking at me. She shakes her head again.

"I know," I laugh. "I didn't know that was possible. I wonder how much smog and pollution we've been breathing back home."

"Might not be 'back home' for long," she grins. "Audrey seems to like it here."

"*You* seem to like it here."

She laughs. "I do, I have to admit it. It's only been a couple days, but I could see myself living here."

A lot of people might balk at the idea of their mother moving to a small town with them, but the thought makes me smile. Audrey loves her, and it would break my heart to leave my mother in Seattle on her own.

"I might miss the ocean, though," she adds, glancing at the mountains. "I've lived on the west coast for the past forty years."

"I thought I would too, but I don't," I tell her, following her eyes to stare at the rough peaks that surround us. "It's comfortable being here. I can't explain it."

Audrey reappears with a full bag of candy in her hand. She's got a gummy in her mouth and she grins at me.

"Audrey!" I exclaim. "I said one piece of candy!"

"It was a mystery bag! I couldn't open it before I bought it!"

I look at my daughter and shake my head. If anyone could find a loophole in what I say, it's her. I sigh, but I can't keep the grin from my face. She extends the bag to me and I hesitate and then laugh and take a piece of candy from the bag. "Thanks," I say.

"You're welcome," Audrey answers, skipping down the sidewalk as my mother and I exchange a glance.

"Well, hello there!" comes a familiar voice. "What's your name?"

I look up and see a woman crouching in front of Audrey. Audrey proudly tells the woman her name and extends a sticky hand for her to shake. The woman glances up at me and I recognize her immediately. It's Mrs. McCoy. Her eyes narrow and a strange smile appears on her lips.

"Nice to meet you, Audrey," she says, not looking at my daughter. "I know your mother."

Mrs. McCoy stands up and walks toward me. An icy chill passes down my spine, and I feel my mother stiffen beside me.

"Welcome to Lang Creek," Margaret McCoy says as she drags her eyes away from mine and looks at my mother. "I'm Margaret."

"Bernadette," my mother answers. I notice she doesn't tell Margaret to call her Bernie, which is unusual. I clear my throat.

"How long are you in town?" I ask, trying to sound casual. Margaret swings those dark eyes back to me and smiles again. She takes a deep breath and shrugs before glancing back at Audrey. The look makes me want to throttle her right here, in full daylight on Main Street.

"Oh, I don't know," she says with a lazy wave of her hand. "I might end up staying for good. It's nice to be home."

"Well, it was nice seeing you again," I respond, making a move to walk around her.

"And nice to meet you," my mother adds, doing the same.

"Yes. Nice to meet you too. Give my regards to Ethan," she says. When she says Ethan's name, it sounds like she spits it out with disgust. I look up to see her eyes flashing with anger. Her lip curls into a snarl and she lifts an eyebrow. "And congratulations on the promotion."

"I... right. Okay, thanks," I stutter, shuffling past her.

"Tell that boyfriend of yours not to start any more fires."

I turn around and stare at the woman as my jaw drops. A smug look appears on her face and she puts her hands on her hips. My mother pauses with me, looking back at the woman. I wonder if she can hear my heartbeat. It's drumming in my chest and filling my ears with the sound of my pulse. Margaret McCoy is looking at me triumphantly and I take a deep breath.

I want to ask her what she means by that. I want to ask her why she spat Ethan's name with disgust. Alarm bells start going off in my head.

He didn't have anything to do with the fire. As long as I keep reminding myself of that, then all these small-town rumors about him won't hold any weight. I close my mouth again and turn around, walking down the street without looking back.

We walk in silence for a full block before my mother speaks.

"Who was that?"

"Mara's mom," I answer, not looking at my mother. I take a deep breath and try to let the crisp air of the mountains clean me after that interaction.

"How did she know about your promotion? And she seemed to know who I was before I even said it."

I shake my head. "I don't know. Ethan doesn't like her."

"What did she mean about the fire?"

I take a deep breath. "There's a rumor that Ethan and his brothers started a fire here last year." My mother grunts, and I look over to see her frowning.

"The fire last year? The fire that's the reason why you're here?"

"Yeah," I reply. "That fire."

"The Ethan that I met yesterday? But he was so sweet!"

"I don't believe the talk!" I add. I glance at Audrey, who is over by a tree, watching a squirrel jump from branch to branch. In a low voice, I keep going. "Ethan told me they were just rumors, and I believe him."

My mother glances back toward Mrs. McCoy and then at me. She takes a deep breath and shakes her head.

"I don't like that woman," she finally says.

I laugh, but there's no humor in it. "Me neither, Mom," I say. "Me neither."

26

ETHAN

FOR THE NEXT WEEK, it seems like everywhere I go, Margaret McCoy is there. I see her at the store, and at Harold's Pub. I run into her when I visit Dominic, clutching his baby and shooting daggers with her eyes. I even see her on a trail by the river when I go out walking one evening.

I just can't get away from her.

Every time I see her, my jaw clenches and I look away. She'll stare at me with that gloating look of hers, and we won't say a word to each other.

She doesn't have to speak, because her face says a thousand words.

I know what you did, it says. *And now I can hurt you with it.*

She knows that I care about Zoe. Everyone knows. It's been obvious since the first day she walked into the office. Even if we'd wanted to hide our relationship, we wouldn't have been able to.

This morning, on my way to work, Margaret McCoy is at convenience store when I go in to grab a coffee before work.

"Ethan Clarke," she says, glancing at me as I walk up to the cash register. "Fancy seeing you here."

I look at her and then up at the cashier. "Thanks, Ted," I tell him with a nod. He grunts, and glances at Margaret.

She's still staring at me. I turn toward her, and suddenly the frustration of the past week is boiling over. I'm sick of seeing her face, jeering at me every time she sees me. I'm sick of feeling like I'm walking on eggshells. I'm sick of being scared of what she'll say to Zoe... or what she'll do.

So in this moment, I'm mad. I stand up straight and stare at Mrs. McCoy, almost for the first time since she's arrived.

"What do you want, Margaret?" I spit. Her thin lips curl into a grin. For the first time, I notice the lines around her eyes and mouth, and the frizzy, greying hair on her head. Her eyes are sharp, but there's an edge to her movements that I've never noticed before.

Still grinning, she takes a step toward me and raises her eyebrows. She opens her mouth, her voice barely above a whisper.

"I want to ruin your life, Ethan," she snarls. "Just like you and your brothers ruined mine."

I snort. "You did that to yourself, Margaret. That had nothing to do with me."

"You ruined my marriage," she spits.

"You did that yourself, as well," I say, a little louder. My heart is thumping. "You're the one who was unfaithful to your husband. I had nothing to do with that. Do you know that he thanked my brothers and me? After you left and he recovered from the shock of finding out his wife had been cheating on him for years with *my own father*, he *thanked* me. What does that tell you?"

Her mouth falls open in shock but she recovers quickly. "Your father didn't seem to mind that I was cheating on my husband. But then again, he was reaping the rewards, wasn't he? How does it feel to know your father was an adulterer?"

"Fuck you, Margaret. Go back to the hole that you crawled out of and get out of my life."

I turn to leave and I hear her cackling behind me. "I'm only getting started, Ethan! We'll see how much that little girl-friend of yours loves you when she finds out who you *really* are."

I glance at Ted, behind the counter, who listened to our whole exchange. He raises an eyebrow and then turns away. I grab my coffee off the counter and storm out the door, the bells above the entrance jingling merrily as I walk out, like they're mocking me.

My truck is parked nearby, and I slam the door as I get in. I'm panting as if I've just sprinted a hundred-yard dash. My heart is racing and my entire head feels like it's burning up. I put my coffee down in the cup holder and put my hands on the steering wheel, squeezing it until my knuckles turn white. I lay my head down on the steering wheel and take a few long, wheezing breaths to try to calm down.

Margaret McCoy is back, and she's out for blood. She can't get to Dominic, because he's with Mara. They have a new daughter, and Margaret seems to care for the baby. At least, it looks that way.

She can't go after Bill, because, well, he's the Sheriff. How do you go up against him?

But that leaves me. I'm the easiest target for her, and she knows it. I burned down the hotel, along with Dominic and Bill, and that was the beginning of the end for her. It was the end of her business success, the end of her marriage, the end of her family.

And now, she wants to end it all for me, too.

I drag the air in and out of my lungs to try to calm down. My thoughts fly to Zoe, and for the thousandth time I regret telling her I didn't have anything to do with the fire. My lie hangs over my head like a black cloud, and I can't seem to bridge the distance between us because of it.

With another deep breath, I try to calm down. Margaret has no proof. Zoe believed me when I said that I had nothing to do with it, so why would one old woman change that? The whole town has turned its back on Mrs. McCoy, so I should be safe.

Should being the operative word.

I jump when someone knocks on my window. Bill Whittaker, the Sheriff, is standing outside my window. I roll it down and nod to him.

"Hey, Bill."

"Ethan," he says, glancing behind me at the convenience store. "Everything okay? You stormed out of there pretty fast."

"Margaret McCoy," I say as way of explanation.

Bill grunts, hooking his thumbs into his belt loops. His eyes darken and he glances at the building again, narrowing his eyes.

"Any idea why she came back?"

He swings his eyes back to me and I lean back in my seat, dropping my hands to my thighs. I take a deep breath and exhale loudly, shaking my head and closing my eyes.

"Yeah," I finally answer. "I do."

Bill waits a moment and then leans against my door. "Care to share?"

I open my eyes again and look at the man who committed arson with my brother and me. If he feels any remorse, he's never shown it in the year that has passed since the fire. I stare into his eyes and finally say the one word that can explain Margaret McCoy's presence in our sleepy little town:

"Revenge."

27

ZOE

Ethan has been different lately, and I don't know if it's because Audrey and my mom are here, or if it's because Margaret McCoy is in town. There's a distance between us that wasn't there before. He's quieter than he was before, and sometimes he doesn't quite meet my eye. I'm trying to give him time to adjust, but it's starting to drive me nuts.

It's early evening, and the sun is starting to set. Ethan, Audrey, and I are walking along the wooded path by the river. It's quiet, and it would be peaceful if I couldn't sense Ethan ruminating beside me.

"It's getting colder in the evenings," I remark placidly, taking a deep breath of crisp air. "Winter's on its way."

"Mm," is the only response I get. We're coming to a bend in the path, and I recognize the spot where Ethan and I made love in the forest the night little Hailey was born, almost two and a half months ago. I pause, glancing out through the break in the trees at the freezing cold water in front of us.

Ethan stares at the river but I can tell his mind is elsewhere. As I watch him, my heart squeezes and fear starts creeping into my heart.

What am I doing? I'm about to accept a promotion to move my entire family across the country. Am I doing it for the promotion? Am I doing it to show Audrey a better, quieter life?

Or... Am I doing it for him?

Maybe I'm just selfish, and not only that, I've been lying to myself. Maybe all I want is a bit of companionship. And now that I've had a taste of it, reality and all its complications are looming in front of me.

Maybe this was a bad idea.

Ethan inhales sharply and seems to come back to the present. He looks at me as if he's seeing me for the first time, reaching over to tuck a strand of hair behind my ear. He leans over and kisses my forehead, sliding his arm across my back and holding me close.

I breathe in and smell wood smoke and pine trees in his chest. I close my eyes and wrap my arms around him and we hold each other without saying a word.

Finally, after a couple minutes, he pulls away and looks into my eyes. His lips curl into a tentative smile and he touches his forehead to mine.

"I'm happy I met you," he says in a low voice.

My heart melts. Or maybe it expands and flips in my chest. I don't know what my heart is doing but whatever it is, it feels good.

"Really?" My voice comes out just above a squeak.

"Really."

It's all the reassurance I need. He presses his lips to mine and kisses me. It might be the thousandth time we've kissed since we met, but it feels more intimate than ever before. He holds me close and runs his fingers through my hair until we stop kissing and I rest my head against his chest. His arms are wrapped around me and I can feel the heat of his body through his jacket.

It feels like there are so many things we should say to each other. I should ask him what he thinks of Audrey, and how he feels about having her in his life all of a sudden. I should ask him what he thinks of my mother, and how he feels about having *her* in his life all of a sudden. It's a big change for all of us.

I should ask him about Mrs. McCoy and all the brooding he's been doing since she got here.

But I don't ask anything. I just lay my head against his chest and listen to the river and the wind in the trees, and the beating of his heart.

After a few minutes, I pull away and look over my shoulder.

"Where's Audrey?" I ask.

Ethan tenses in my arm and looks around. We separate and head down the path. The blood drains from my face and my chest suddenly feels hollow.

"Audrey?" I call out into the forest. Somehow, the sky has turned darker and dusk has almost turned to night. I walk a little faster, and then start jogging as my calls become more and more frantic. Ethan calls her name as well, yelling it into the trees. He ducks down near the river and comes back up, shaking his head.

"How far could she have gone? If she gets lost..." The words hang between us and I call out for Audrey again.

There's another bend in the path up ahead. My vision is blurred as my eyes start to fill with tears. "Audrey!" I call out. "Answer me!"

My voice is strained and the panic is gripping my throat. *Where is she?*

Then, I see her blue jacket appear from a tiny dirt path on the left. "Mom!" She says, beaming. "Look what I made!"

"Audrey!" I say in relief, wrapping my arms around her in a tight hug. I trap her arms by her sides and hold her tighter than I should, until she squirms and I let her go. She looks at me and frowns.

"Are you okay, Mom?"

Ethan comes up behind us and I hear him make a noise. "What the fuck are you doing here?" he spits. I tense, and Audrey inhales at his swear word, widening her eyes. I follow his eyes to the woman standing in the trees where Audrey just appeared.

"I'm out for a walk, Ethan," Margaret McCoy says haughtily. "Is that allowed, or do I need the Clarke seal of approval for that?"

Ethan tenses, and I stand up and move Audrey behind me, putting myself between her and Mrs. McCoy. Margaret sighs.

"I came across Audrey on the path and I showed her how to make boats out of sticks to race down the river," she says, almost as if she's bored. She gestures to Audrey, who holds up her creation. "She was on her own out here."

My stomach falls and my cheeks burn. *She was on her own out here.* Margaret looks at me accusingly as she says it. I should have been with her. Instead, I was wrapped in Ethan's arms, with no thought at all for my daughter.

Margaret gives me a look of pure disgust and gestures to the path behind us. "May I?" she says.

Ethan steps aside and Margaret starts walking. She turns to Audrey and waves. "Hope you make a really fast stick-boat," she says with a smile. "Remember the trick I taught you for tying the ends of it?"

Audrey smiles and holds up her boat. "I'll make a really good one and show it to you next time."

Margaret smiles, and for the first time I see a softness in her eyes. She nods. "That sounds good. You take care now, and don't wander away from your mother anymore."

If everyone in town hadn't warned me about Margaret McCoy, I'd almost think she was a nice person right now.

But Ethan obviously doesn't think so. He doesn't relax until she's out of sight, and then the dark cloud above his head reappears. The tender moment we shared before is forgotten, and the three of us head back toward town in silence. I hold Audrey's hand, and she stares at her new creation the whole time.

When we get back to town, I send Audrey over to our car and I turn to Ethan.

"Why do you hate her so much?"

His eyebrows shoot up, and then his face darkens. He shakes his head. "You wouldn't understand."

"Try me."

He chews his lip and finally sighs. "She stole my father's business after he died, so my brothers and I were left with nothing. We found out later that they were having an affair. My dad and Margaret," he explains. I try to hide the surprise from my face, but Ethan laughs grimly. "Yeah. That was my reaction as well. Dominic started seeing Mara, and she did everything she could to keep them apart."

"Oh," I say. I can't think of a better response.

Ethan straightens up and puts his hands on my shoulders, running them down to hold both my hands. He looks me in the eyes. "She's not a good person, Zoe," he says. "She had everyone fooled for years. But at the first chance, she just threw everyone around her under the bus and took care of herself. Including her own daughter."

A lump forms in my throat and I think of the look on Margaret's face when she said goodbye to Audrey. Could she really have been cruel enough to her own daughter to keep Mara and Dominic apart?

"No good will come of her being here," Ethan continues. He sighs again and I put my hands on either side of his face.

"Try not to worry so much," I tell him with a smile. "I'm just glad you're not freaking out about Audrey and my mom being here."

Confusion passes over his face and he frowns. "What? Why would I be freaking out?"

I laugh and shake my head. "Never mind. I have an overactive imagination. I'll see you tomorrow."

I pull his head toward mine and kiss him tenderly. He wraps his arms around me and I feel at ease. I hear my car door open and Audrey's voice behind me.

"*Eeewww,*" she yells. "Gross!"

Both Ethan and I laugh, and he winks at me. "See you tomorrow," he whispers. With one last kiss on the tip of my nose, he turns toward his vehicle, and I turn toward mine.

28

———

ETHAN

I'M on my own today for the first time in a long time. Zoe is visiting the school with Audrey, and they're having a quiet dinner together. It's finally Friday, and when I get home from work, I feel the restless itch to get out of my house. I take a quick shower and head over to Harold's for a beer. When I walk into the bar, the din of voices and glasses and music assails me but it feels almost comforting.

Harold plops a beer in front of me as soon as I sit down. "On the house, Clarke. Looks like you need it." He laughs, and I nod in thanks. I didn't think I looked that bad, but I'll take the beer anyway.

I'm halfway through drinking it when Bill Whittaker sits down beside me.

"Ethan," he says with a nod.

"Sheriff," I answer.

"Off-duty," he retorts.

"You're still the Sheriff though."

"So I am," he grins. Harold places his drink in front of him and Bill holds up his glass. "You know what today is?"

I shake my head, touching my glass to his.

"Today is eighteen months since we torched that fucking hotel to the ground."

I glance around us. "Keep your voice down, Bill, come on," I say in a low voice. Bill laughs, hand on stomach and head thrown back. He takes a long drink and claps me on the back.

"You just said it, Ethan. I'm the Sheriff!"

"You're insane," I grin. "I'm glad you're on my side."

"Oh, I don't take sides." There's a sparkle in his eye and I raise an eyebrow.

"No?"

"No. I just do what's best for the town."

"Right."

"Just so happens you, your brothers, and I agreed on that particular occasion."

"Lucky for us."

"Lucky for us," he agrees with a grin. "Come on, cheer up, Ethan. What's bothering you? I haven't seen you this moody since before your girlfriend came to town."

"Moody!"

"Yeah, you moody fucker," he chuckles, clapping me on the back again. "Worse than my mother-in-law."

"Couldn't be that bad."

"Gettin' close!"

I laugh, finally, and Bill looks triumphant. I finish my beer and wave for another one, and soon Bill and I are as comfortable as we've always been. I don't think about Margaret, or Zoe, or anything. It's just me and my buddy, having a beer on a Friday evening. It's nice.

He starts telling me about the teenagers he caught spray-painting the bridge just outside of town.

"Those little fuckers are quick, let me tell you," he says, shaking his head. "But I was quicker. Thinkin' of changing my name to Usain."

I laugh. "Sheriff Bolt has a nice ring to it."

Bill winks at me and I shake my head. Maybe he's right, maybe I have been moody. Ever since Margaret McCoy came to town, I've been worried about her motives. Maybe my moodiness was why Zoe thought I didn't like Audrey and her mom.

"So what do you figure about Margaret McCoy coming back?" Bill says almost too casually. My jaw immediately tenses and I stare into my glass.

"I don't know what's she's up to, but I don't like it."

Bill grunts in agreement. "What do Mara and Dominic think about it?"

"They're tolerating it, I think. She's playing the grandmother card with the new baby." I take a deep breath and shake my head in frustration.

Bill grunts again. We both take a sip in silence.

"You think she'll cause trouble?" Bill asks.

It's my turn to grin. "You're the Sheriff, Bill, you'll sort her out if she does."

He laughs again. "Fuckin' right I will."

The door at the entrance of the pub opens and I see both my brothers walk in. I wave them over and they nod, heading toward Bill and me. Soon, the four of us are drinking and laughing like old times. By the end of my third beer, my shoulders relax. I didn't know my eyebrows were drawn together until the tension in my forehead is gone.

Aiden tells a story about Dominic when we were kids, and soon the two of them are jostling with each other semi-playfully. Harold throws ice cubes at them from behind the bar.

"Cut it out, you savages! If you break another one of my chairs, I swear to God…"

Aiden laughs and puts Dominic in a head lock. "We're just playing, Harry."

"Well, play somewhere else," he says, throwing another ice cube. Dominic laughs and extricates himself from Aiden's hold. He finishes his beer and nods at Harold for another one. Harold purses his lips but grabs another glass and pours a fresh drink. There's a gleam in his eye when he puts the glass down in front of Dominic.

Before I know it, Dominic makes a move to leave. "Got to get home to the baby," he says, and Aiden follows his lead with a grunt. Bill isn't too far behind.

Soon, I'm left on my own. My thoughts drift back to Zoe. All three of them–Bill, Aiden, Dominic–they all have wives and kids to go home to. And here I am, staring at half a glass of beer.

I'd love it if Zoe were here with me, or if she were at home when I got there. I'd love to wake up next to her every morning. And the more I get to know Audrey and Bernie, the more I like them. I never thought I'd date a single mother but having them in my life has made me change the way I think.

I finish the last of my beer and pay Harry before pushing myself up off the bar stool and heading out the door. For the rest of the night, when I walk home and lie in bed, all I'm thinking of is Zoe.

My brothers love Zoe, their wives love Zoe. Everyone in town seems to have taken to her. Without either of us noticing, she's become part of this community. She's become part of *my life*.

I turn over in bed and look at the empty space beside me, wishing she were here.

If she accepts the position, and she and Audrey and Bernie move to Lang Creek, they'll need a place to stay.

I close my eyes and take a deep breath. Would she... would she want to move in with me? The thought fills me with fear and excitement and makes my heart feel like it's almost too big for my chest. When I open my eyes again, I stare at the ceiling and feel my lips pulling up into a smile.

It might be the beers, but I don't think it is. I want Zoe to be part of my life. I want her here beside me. I want her to move in with me, and I want to watch Audrey grow up. I want to have Thanksgiving and Christmas dinners with Bernie and my brothers. Having Zoe beside me feels like the most natural thing to ever happen, and the thought of living with her feels right.

I'm not sure when it happened, but somehow, I feel like I've gained a family with them. I sigh and turn over in my bed, stretching my arm out to where Zoe would be if she were here.

I've turned into a big softie, that's what's happened. I just never thought it would feel this good.

29

ZOE

"Do you have everything you need, Audrey?" I ask, throwing an apple into her lunchbox and zipping it up. She appears in the doorway between the bathroom and the bedroom, backpack on and shoes tied.

"I'm ready! And don't worry, Mom!" She says. "I'll be fine."

"I know you will, monkey," I say, handing her the lunchbox and walking with her to the hotel lobby. I've started viewing apartments and houses around town for us to move into, hoping to get out of this hotel room by the end of the week. I don't have many options, but Katie and Mara are helping me contact people who might have a place for us to rent. There isn't much in the way of real estate agents in this town.

Audrey skips along beside me and we wait at the bus stop together. I check the time on my phone, anxious to see the big yellow bus coming around the bend. Another mother with her child appears, and Audrey looks a bit apprehensive, and my heart squeezes.

The little boy looks at her and smiles. "Hi."

"Hi," Audrey responds.

"I like your backpack."

"Thanks," she says. "I like yours, too."

"It has a secret pocket–look!" The boy says, showing off his bag proudly. Audrey laughs and soon she's engrossed in a conversation. I smile, and for the first time since I got this promotion, I feel like I might have made the right decision. Audrey seems to like it here, and she hasn't mentioned the mean girls at her old school in Seattle since she left.

I nod to the mother and smile, watching my daughter and feeling my heart swell. Before long, the bus comes around the bend and I send her off. I let out a big sigh as the doors close and Audrey waves at me through the window.

"The first day of school never really gets any easier, does it?" the other mother says. I glance at her and chuckle, shaking my head.

"Sometimes I think it's easier for them than it is for us."

"Oh, there's no question about it," she laughs. "It's absolutely easier for them."

By the time I get to work, my nerves seem to have calmed down. They've given me an office in the back of the building to go along with my promotion, and I'm starting to contact other rangers in the area. I'll have a couple National Parks to look after in this job, which means more work than I've ever had before.

A soft knock on the door makes me look up. Sandy looks in, smiling.

"Morning," she says, and her stern features soften. "How's the new office?"

"It's perfect, Sandy, thank you," I reply.

"You settling in okay?"

"I... actually, yeah. Audrey went off to school today, and my mother is down in the next town doing a pottery class. I think they're finding this easier than I am."

Sandy chuckles. "That's always how it is." She stares off through the window for a moment and then turns back to me. "I heard you were looking for a place to stay," she says. I glance at her, eyebrows shooting up. I nod. "Well, I don't have anything for you and Audrey, but I do have a one-bedroom cabin on my property. I've rented it out once or twice, but mostly I just use it for family who come to visit. I know you said your mother likes gardening, and there's a little veggie patch out back. She can come have a look to see if she'd like it."

Sandy is glancing at me with her eyebrows drawn and she's wringing her hands in front of her. She looks almost nervous and my jaw drops as my heart grows in my chest. The thoughtfulness of the townspeople here will never cease to surprise me. I smile and dip my chin down.

"I think she'd like that," I respond. "I'll let her know tonight and we can set up a viewing."

Sandy smiles, and I wonder how I ever thought she was stern. "It would be nice to have another woman my age to talk to," she says. "Bernie seems wonderful."

"Thank you, Sandy," I say. When she turns around and leaves my new office, I lean back in my chair and let out a big breath. Lang Creek is feeling more and more like home to me.

When evening comes, I tell Sandy I'll be over with my mother later and I head off to the hotel. Ethan and I have plans for dinner, so my mother, Audrey, Ethan, and I end up walking over to Sandy's house in the early evening. Ethan slips his hand into mine as we walk, and Audrey skips ahead.

I don't know if it's the cool autumn wind that blows through my hair, or maybe it's the two glasses of wine that I've had, but my heart flutters in my chest. My mother is humming to herself, and she looks up at the mountains and smiles.

Somehow, everyone is happy. We've slipped into a new life without too much fuss, and the stress of our life back in Seattle has mostly disappeared.

Sandy's cabin is lovely, and my mother agrees to rent it out on the spot. Before long, she and Sandy are discussing the intricacies of the veggie patch. After some time, all five of us head off for a short walk in the forest. I lean my head against Ethan's shoulder as I listen to Sandy explain the ins and outs of soil composition for vegetable growing, or something of the sort. Audrey runs up ahead, inspecting bugs and picking up sticks as we walk.

Without me realizing it, in the past few weeks all my worries have turned out to be baseless, and I'm actually *happy*. We walk until we get to a small grassy area by the river. Ethan, my mother, Sandy, and I sit on benches as Audrey walks down to the water's edge. I watch her pick up sticks and nimbly weave them together to make a watercraft, and I smile.

Maybe Mrs. McCoy wasn't so bad. At least Audrey's getting some use out of her new skills. Ethan puts his arm around my shoulder and squeezes me closer, and I turn toward him. He lays his lips over mine and I shiver in contentment. Vaguely, I can hear Sandy and Mom deep in conversation about carrots and tomatoes, but all my attention is on Ethan.

He wraps me in his arms and runs his fingers along my cheek. He kisses me tenderly and then leans his forehead against mine. I close my eyes for a moment.

"Move in with me."

His words are barely above a whisper, but I open my eyes and stare at him. "What?" I ask, heart thumping.

"I mean it. You've looked at half a dozen places and none of them were good for you and Audrey. I live near the bus stop, and she'll be able to walk to the town's soccer field and basketball courts. It's a great location for you as well, near work, and–"

I start laughing as he babbles, and he stops talking to look at me, confused. My eyes soften and I put my hands on either side of his face.

"You would do that for us?"

It's his turn to chuckle. "I'm doing it for *me*, Zoe. I want you with me. I want Audrey with us. You make me happy."

My heart grows so much it feels like it's going to burst out of my chest. My eyes start to mist and his face goes blurry, so all I can do is nod my head up and down. My voice is gone, and there's a lump in my throat. I don't need to say anything, though, because Ethan crushes his lips against mine and wraps his arms around me. My heart sings for him, and I kiss him fiercely. What have I done to be so lucky?

We kiss until nothing else matters, and I forget where I am.

I forget where I am until a gargled scream pulls me back to the present. My stomach drops and my head whips around to where Audrey was standing. I see my mother move faster than I've ever seen before, sprinting toward the river and jumping to where my daughter's head has just disappeared under the water's surface.

Ethan jumps up, yelling at my mother to stop but she doesn't listen. My voice is gone, and all I can do is run toward the two people I love most with my heart in my throat and panic coursing through my veins. The water splashes as I watch my mom jump in and dread grips my entire body like a cold hand. My eyes flick to the center of the river, where the icy water is rushing dangerously fast.

I watch in a daze as Ethan grabs a long stick, running toward the bank of the river. My mother is swimming with long, powerful strokes, and finally a scream rips out of my throat. My scream hits my ears as if it's coming from another world, and the anguish tears at my chest. My feet are in the water and Ethan is yelling at me to stand back.

My mom is diving down, and after three or four agonizing seconds, she reappears with my daughter in her arm. Ethan splashes in the water to his thighs and extends the stick toward her. She grabs onto it and I watch him pull both of them back to safety.

I'm still screaming. Audrey's lips and skin are an unnatural shade of blue. My mother is shivering. Ethan is saying something, but I can't understand anything. I wrap them in my arms and I cry and cry and cry until powerful arms pull me away and drag the three of us back toward town.

30

―――――

ETHAN

THIS IS MY FAULT. If I hadn't been so caught up with kissing Zoe, I would have noticed Audrey walking on the slippery rocks on the edge of the river. I could have called her back, and none of this would have happened. I try to forget the chilling scream that came from Zoe when she saw Audrey disappear under the water's surface. My hands tighten on the steering wheel and I glance at the two of them in the back seat. Zoe is rubbing Audrey's body, whispering to her and crying as we race down the highway toward the hospital.

I look back at the road, trying to ignore the memory of my own father's death. It was eerily similar, except it was Mara McCoy that fell in the river, and my father that jumped in after her. He refused to be treated at the hospital, the stubborn fool, and got pneumonia. By the time we got help for him a few days later, it was too late.

Now, the nightmare that plagued me for years is happening again. My heart is splitting in two for Zoe. I never knew I could care so much about someone, but I do. I glance in the mirror again and the pain in my heart hardens.

This isn't my fault. This is Margaret McCoy's fault. I don't know how she's done it, but somehow, she's caused this. She showed Audrey how to build those stupid stick boats. She planted the seed of fascination with the rushing, icy water of the river. The fury builds in my stomach until I can't see anything except the road in front of me. I tighten my grip on the steering wheel until I think it might snap.

I can see Sandy's car in the rear-view mirror. She's got Bernie with her, and our little convoy is breaking every road law there is to get them to the hospital.

Zoe sobs in the back seat and the vice grip around my heart tightens.

"It'll be okay, Zoe," I hear myself say. "We're almost there."

"I should have been watching her," she says, rocking back and forth. "I was so fucking happy and selfish."

"It was an accident," I say through gritted teeth, knowing exactly how she feels because I feel the same way. "It's no one's fault." Even as I say the words, anger flashes through me.

We get to the hospital and it doesn't take long for Audrey and Bernie to be rushed into a room together. The nurses tell Zoe in no uncertain terms to step aside, and I put my arm around her shoulders to lead her away. She's shivering and watching the medical team work through wide, blood-shot eyes. Tears are falling down her cheeks and I doubt she even notices them drip off her chin.

I glance at Sandy, who purses her lips and watches the nurses and doctors try to warm the two patients up.

Just when I thought I was gaining a family, they're being ripped away from me. My eyes fill with tears and I squeeze Zoe closer to try to distract myself from the pain in my heart. Zoe feels so frail in my arms, and she leans on me for support.

"I'll get a couple coffees," Sandy says. "Take her to sit down over there."

For once, I welcome Sandy's stern commands. She's the one who took control of the situation by the river, telling me to grab Zoe and Audrey as she picked up Bernie as if she weighed no more than a child. She's the one who told me to drive to the hospital, and she's the one who spoke to the doctors. She's been the voice of reason, and now, once again, I listen to her.

I guide Zoe to a seat and wrap my arms around her, whispering everything and nothing into her ear as she stares off into space.

Sandy reappears and hands us two steaming Styrofoam cups of coffee. It tastes terrible. Zoe doesn't even try hers. She just sits next to me and stares at the floor.

"I was so focused on that stupid veggie patch," Sandy says, glancing down the hall toward Audrey and Bernie. "I didn't even know what was happening until Bernie was halfway to the river."

Zoe makes a strangled noise and Sandy crouches in front of her. My boss only looks like that when something has gone wrong at work and she needs to take control of a bad situation. Her usually impeccable grey hair is falling out of her bun, and the lines on her face are deeper than usual. She puts her coffee down on the floor and places both hands on Zoe's thighs.

"Now you listen to me, Randall," she commands. Zoe's eyes widen and she stiffens beside me. "Your daughter is going to be fine. These are great doctors, and she was only in the water for a minute. You hear me? She's going to be *fine*."

"I'm a terrible mother," Zoe says. Her voice is flat, and she doesn't seem to know where she is.

"Oh, hush," Sandy says. "You're a wonderful mother. Everyone can see it. Now you need to be the great mother that you are and be ready to be strong for your family. You hear me?"

That seems to have some effect on Zoe. She sits up a bit straighter and wipes her eyes on the back of her hand. She nods to Sandy, taking a sip of coffee before grimacing.

Sandy chuckles. "Worst coffee I've ever had," she agrees, standing up and glancing down the hall.

SANDY STAYS with us until the early hours of the morning. She nods off on a chair at one point, but she's there, with us, the whole time. Zoe seems to come around after a couple hours and tells Sandy to go home. Sandy laughs. "You won't get rid of me that easily," she says, and that's that.

Every minute is agony and every hour is endless. I try to stop my mind from drifting back to that day by the river over a decade ago, when my father did the same thing for Mara McCoy. It was the start of the decade-long feud between the McCoys and the Clarkes that tore this town in half. Now, I'm reliving that nightmare and somehow it feels even more visceral.

Finally, a tired-looking doctor appears and nods to us.

"Audrey is going to be fine," he says unceremoniously. Zoe makes a horrible strangled sound and immediately starts sobbing. The doctor nods, waiting for her to compose herself before continuing. "Bernadette is still in critical condition," he says. Zoe makes another horrible noise and I put my arm around her shoulders.

"Can we see them?" I ask. The doctor nods, and leads us down the stark white hallway to their room. It smells like antiseptic and the fluorescent lights are giving me a headache. Zoe's shaking.

Zoe goes to Audrey, climbing in the bed beside her and putting her arm gently over her daughter's body. She puts her head next to the pillow and cries silently as Audrey sleeps. The color is returning to the girl's cheeks and lips, and Sandy squeezes my arm as she lets out a sigh of relief.

I glance at the next bed, where Bernie is laying. She looks pale as a nurse attends to her. She has thermal blankets over her entire body, and the nurse is jotting down her vital signs on a chart. I pull up a chair between the two beds and find Bernie's hand, holding it in my own. It's cold. Memories flood my mind and for a moment, I see my father laying on his death bed in this same hospital.

"Don't die," I whisper to her. "Please, Bernie, don't die."

31

ZOE

MY MOTHER DIES in that hospital bed. She's too old and too frail to sustain that kind of shock to her system. The doctors aren't able to get her body temperature back to where it should be, and she never wakes up.

I'm numb.

She passes as I hold her hand and Audrey sleeps in the bed next to her. The pain in my heart is indescribable. The mix of guilt and shame and misery swirling around inside me feels like a thousand cuts to the flesh, slowly bleeding as I watch my mother breathe her last breath.

She saved my daughter and it cost her her life. Ethan and Sandy are beside me, but I don't see them. I just see my mother and her eerily pale skin, the peaceful look on her face and the eyes that will never again sparkle as she laughs.

I think Ethan puts his hand on my shoulder at one point, but I'm not sure. I just sit there and look at my mother's body until the pain inside me is almost too much to bear.

Sandy says something about not worrying about coming to work, and Ethan says something else, but I don't hear any of it. One of them puts a jacket over my shoulders and some food appears beside me, but nothing makes me move from my seat next to my mother's bed.

It's not until I hear Audrey's voice behind me that I'm pulled out of my stupor. What she says breaks my heart all over again.

"I'm sorry, Mommy," she says in a whisper. "My boat was getting stuck in the rocks and I just wanted it to float down the river."

I turn to my daughter and shake my head, wrapping her in my arms. "Shh, Audrey. It's not your fault. I'm just glad you're okay."

"What happened? Where's Grandma?"

My heart breaks all over again and I take a deep breath. This is one of the hardest things I've ever had to do, but I look in my daughter's eyes and brush a strand of hair off her face.

"Your grandmother was very brave. She ran into the water to get you out. She saved you from the river, and she's the most amazing woman I've ever known."

Audrey glances over at the other bed. "Is she asleep?"

It's hard to speak with the lump that's formed in my throat, and I can see the wheels turning in Audrey's head. She looks at me and then at her grandmother again, and her face scrunches in fear. Her eyes widen and my heart feels like it's shattering all over again.

"Will she wake up?" Her voice is a squeak, and mine is completely gone. All I can do is shake my head from side to side and hold my sobbing daughter to my chest. We cry together, and Audrey just keeps repeating *I'm sorry, Mommy. I'm sorry. I'm sorry.*

I pull away from her and take her face in my hands. "This is not your fault, Audrey. Do you hear me? It was an accident. Your grandmother died to save your life, and I will forever be grateful." My voice catches on the last word, and I take a deep breath. "It is *not* your fault."

"Of course it's my fault," Audrey says, and I see fear and sorrow in her eyes. "I'm sorry, Mom. You told me not to get too close to the water. I'm so sorry. Grandma..."

"Shh, Audrey," I say, holding her close to me. I try to comfort her but my voice is gone again, and all I can do is rock her gently back and forth.

THE NEXT FEW days are a blur. Ethan takes me home with him, and somehow all my things appear in his house. Food appears in our fridge, and I vaguely realize that almost everyone in town brings us things we might need. We have frozen casseroles and dinners, flowers, drinks, teddy bears. Even Ethan's house gets a spruce up from the endless stream of people coming to help us and give their condolences. Squeaky hinges are fixed, he gets a new dining table and a bed for Audrey's room. The generosity is endless.

I try to be grateful, but it's exhausting. Somewhere, in the deep recesses of my heart, I realize that this community has accepted me as one of their own, but right now I'm just trying to keep breathing. Seconds tick by and the pain doesn't go away.

Audrey recovers from her physical injuries as only children can, but there's a darkness in her eyes that wasn't there before. Her voice is dampened, and I don't see her jump and dance and laugh like she used to. Ethan sees me watching her and puts his hands on my shoulder.

"She'll recover," he says softly into my ear, and I try to blink back the tears in my eyes. I nod vigorously and try to force a smile.

"I know," I answer. I'm just not sure if I will.

Two weeks after the accident, Audrey is recovered enough to go back to school, and I try to contain the heart-wrenching fear in my heart when I watch her leave. It's hard to have her out of my sight, but Ethan squeezes my shoulder and kisses my temple and I let her go.

"Come on," he says after she's gotten on the bus. "Let's get some brunch at the hotel. My treat."

I watch the bus disappear around the bend and ignore the urge to run after it and drag my daughter back to my side. I look at the man who's held me up these past few weeks and nod.

"That sounds nice," I respond, and he squeezes my shoulder again.

"I love you, Zoe," he says matter-of-factly.

"I love you too."

And that's that. We head toward the hotel for some breakfast.

32

———

ETHAN

By the end of September, Zoe, Audrey and I have slipped into a new routine. Lang Creek townspeople start getting excited about the biggest event of the year: The Fall Festival. It seems like everyone is in town for it. I see people here all the way from Long Lake, and even Albany. Even Mickey, who owns the B&B that I like, is here.

I walk hand-in-hand with Zoe, and Audrey skips beside us. Audrey is laughing more. Settling into a routine with school seems to have helped. Zoe still looks sad when she stares off into nothing, but she's starting to laugh again too. We don't talk about that day by the river too much, but it hangs over us like a dark cloud.

Zoe leans into me as we walk, and I squeeze her hand. She's wearing jeans and a tight top with a clingy cardigan, and she couldn't look any better. We walk into the festival grounds, wandering through food stalls and a farmer's market. We stop in front of some performers. One of them is juggling while the other is cracking jokes. Audrey glances up at the two of us with laughter in her eyes before turning back to the performers.

Zoe turns to me and I touch my nose to hers.

"Thank you," she says as I kiss her forehead.

"There's nothing to thank me for," I answer. She smiles and shakes her head, and I see a lightness in her face that I haven't seen in a long, long time. Maybe it's all the people, maybe it's Audrey laughing and skipping in front of us, maybe it's the crisp autumn air. Whatever it is, Zoe looks how she did before the accident. It's been a few weeks now, and the shock of the incident seems to have worn off.

Audrey is doing well at school, and we've settled into a new normal life. I never thought I would say this, but things are *good*.

I kiss Zoe's forehead, thankful that she seems to be coming back to me after the trauma of losing her mother and almost losing Audrey.

"I want to go on the pony!" Audrey says, pointing to a sign for pony rides. There's a large enclosure at the other end of the fair grounds. Zoe nods and smiles, and the three of us set off in the direction of the pony rides.

We're only about halfway there when Margaret McCoy steps out in front of us. I freeze, and Zoe does the same. Audrey smiles at Margaret.

"Hi, Mrs. McCoy!" she calls out.

Zoe bristles, and I wonder if, like me, she resents Margaret and the stick boats that started the horrible chain of events near the river.

"Hi there, Audrey. How are you?"

"I'm fine," she says cheerily, oblivious to our discomfort. "I'm going on a pony ride!"

"Isn't that nice," Margaret says, not looking at Audrey. Her eyes are trained on me, and a chill goes down my spine. I stand up straighter.

"Why are you still here, Margaret?" I ask. "Life was better when you weren't in town."

"Was it, now?" She asks slowly, glancing from me to Zoe and back. Zoe squeezes my hand as if to say, *don't make a scene*. She turns to Zoe. "I'm sorry to hear about your mother. She seemed like a lovely woman."

Zoe tenses. "She was," she answers through gritted teeth.

Margaret smiles, but her eyes remain dull. "Glad you've found a bit of happiness," she says, nodding to me. "Although a Clarke wouldn't be my first choice."

"Oh fuck off, Margaret," I explode. "All you've done here is cause trouble since the day you stepped foot in town. Do you thrive off making people feel uncomfortable?"

Her face turns dark. "This is my town as much as it is yours! I'm sick of you and your brothers parading around town like you own the place. How *dare* you speak to me like that!"

"How dare I?" I repeat, incredulous. "*How dare I?!*"

The anger is rising inside me. Zoe squeezes my hand again but it's like I have tunnel vision. All I can see is Margaret McCoy, and the anger of the last decade starts to flood my veins. I'm vaguely aware that I'm shaking. It takes all my concentration to keep myself in one piece when my body feels like it's about to explode.

She has the nerve to be mad at *me*, when Margaret McCoy is the reason that Audrey was playing near the water. Margaret is the reason that Bernie died. Margaret is the reason that Dominic almost lost Mara last year, and the reason that my brothers and I lost our father's business. *She* is the reason that the past ten years have been spent in a dark hole of depression and misery and scraping by and wondering why life is so difficult when your last name is 'Clarke'.

I slip my hand out of Zoe's and ball my hands into fists. My nails dig into my palms and the pain of it eases the fury in me long enough to notice Dominic at the edge of my vision. People are pausing near us, glancing at us curiously and waiting to see what happens. Their shameless curiosity only angers me more.

I shake my head. "You're evil, Margaret McCoy. Pure evil. You don't care about anyone but yourself. I don't know why you're here, but I know you're up to no good."

"Well, at least I'm not an arsonist," she spits. Zoe tenses beside me but I don't have the energy to look at her. All my focus is on McCoy. I see my brothers moving toward me from the corner of my eye, but the words are already leaving my mouth.

"I'm *glad* I burned that fucking thing down," I spit. "That hotel was just a testament to your greed. You don't care about this town or these mountains. All you care about is yourself. You're probably here to remind everyone that you've ruined at least two families with your spite." I spit the words out. I'm shaking, the heat rising to my ears as I try to contain my anger. I take a step toward her and shake my head. "I'd burn down that fucking hotel a hundred times if it meant you left town and never came back."

It's not until Dominic puts a hand on my chest and makes me step back that I realize how badly I'm trembling. I look up and see a ring of people around us, and Margaret McCoy looking at me with a triumphant look on her face. Dominic sighs, pushing me back gently another step.

"Ethan," he says, and shakes his head.

I turn around and my heart drops.

Zoe's face has a thousand emotions written across it. I can see the pain and betrayal of my words. The lie I told her, months ago, to protect my brothers and my town is coming back to haunt me. Margaret is gloating behind me and Zoe's bottom lip is trembling. The pain in her eyes is indescribable, and my heart rips in half. It feels like two hands are pulling my chest apart, and my insides are spilling onto the ground in front of me.

Zoe doesn't say a word. She looks at me for another second, and then takes Audrey's hand and walks away.

"Zoe, wait!" I call out. I break free from Dominic's grip and run after her. "Wait!"

She stops and glances around at the dozens of people watching us. *Fucking Fall Festival,* I think as I see the mortification in her eyes. Finally, she drags her eyes back up to mine and it feels like a dagger has been plunged right into my heart.

"You lied to me," she says, her voice low and pregnant with emotion. "All this time, you've been lying."

"Zoe, I…"

She holds up a hand and I stop talking. Her eyes shine with unsaid words, and she turns around again, walking away from me.

I want to run after her. I want to drop to my knees in front of her and beg her to forgive me. I want to explain that I lied because I didn't know her. I lied to protect my brother and the Sheriff, to protect my town. I lied to protect myself.

I want to tell her that everything is different now, that I don't want to protect myself from her because I love her. I love her more than I've loved anyone before.

But I can't say anything. I watch her walk away, hand-in-hand with her daughter, and my feet turn concrete. I stay rooted in place as my heart breaks over and over with every step that she takes. It's not until Dominic puts a hand on my shoulder that I tear my eyes away from Zoe.

"I've lost her," I say. My voice is flat, and my whole body feels grey. I'm empty.

"Come on," my brother says. "Let's get out of here."

Numb, I follow him in the opposite direction, glancing one last time in the direction that Zoe left.

33

ZOE

AUDREY'S VOICE sounds like it's a thousand miles away. It's like she's speaking to me from under water. I'm standing outside the festival grounds, looking down the road.

"Mom?" She says gently.

I'm pulled out of my stupor and look at my young daughter. Her face is drawn, with her eyebrows pulled together and her eyes full of concern.

"Are you okay?"

"Of course, Audrey," I lie. "I'm fine."

Where will we go?

Stupidly, I've moved all my things to Ethan's house. I've moved all *Audrey's* things there, too! I've moved her all the way from her home to come to this godforsaken place! A place full of lies and deceit and decades of animosity. *Why* would I willingly come to a place like this? Tears cloud my eyes as I curse myself.

Audrey tugs at my arm and nods toward the McCoy hotel. "Let's go see Katie," she says, and I follow my daughter numbly.

I should be the responsible one right now. I should be the mom. I should be the one telling *her* where we'll go and what we'll do. But all I can do is follow her lead and let my feet take me down Main Street toward the largest building in town. I stumble on the pavement, and Audrey squeezes my hand. Her lips are set in a thin line, and she keeps her eyes trained on the hotel. She looks much, much older than eight years old.

Guilt floods through me and swirls in my stomach with the pain of Ethan's betrayal. If it were just me that was hurt, I could deal with it. But now I've dragged my family along, for what? My mother has died and now Audrey has to deal with her own pain and mine.

I'm a horrible mother. Selfish, short-sighted, and careless. Tears well up in my eyes and I try to blink them away. Audrey stomps beside me, all but pulling me toward the McCoy hotel.

When we get there, she pushes the door open and guides me to a couch in the lobby. She sits down beside me and lays her head on my shoulder. I lift my arm and snuggle her into my side, squeezing her and kissing the top of her head. I inhale the scent of her hair and my heart squeezes again.

She puts her arm on my leg and takes a long, shuddering breath. After a moment, she looks up at me.

"Mom, what happened with the fire?"

My chest squeezes and I shake my head. "Don't worry about that, Audrey. It was before I got here."

"Tell me," she says, and the maturity in her voice surprises and saddens me. "I want to know what happened."

I take a deep breath and glance at her before shaking my head. "I'm not sure, baby."

"I'm not a baby," she says automatically, and I smile. It feels like my face is cracking from the effort, but the weight on my heart lifts just a little.

"No, you're not." I answer, almost to myself. "Well, all I know is that there was a big hotel being built, and people were worried that it would bring lots of people to the area that wouldn't care about the mountains. So some naughty people burned it down."

"Was Ethan one of those naughty people?"

My heart breaks all over again and I try to swallow past the lump in my throat. Finally, I nod. "Yeah. He was."

Audrey is silent for a while. We both turn toward the sound of footsteps and I hurriedly brush the tears from my eyes. I breathe a sigh of relief when Katie appears. Her face is drawn and she rushes toward the two of us.

"I heard what happened," she breathes. "Are you okay?"

"How did you hear what happened already?" I ask, frowning. "We only left a few minutes ago."

Katie looks at me and cocks her head to the side. She grins and shakes her head. "It's Lang Creek, Zoe," she chuckles. "News travels fast."

Her eyes turn to Audrey and she kneels in front of us. She pulls out an envelope from her bag and holds it out toward Audrey. "Can you find Mara and give her this?" she asks in a somber voice. "It's very important. She's in the office."

Audrey is still for a second and then tentatively takes the envelope. She nods once, and then turns to lay a kiss on my cheek. I try to smile at her, and inhale deeply as she walks down the hallway toward the office.

Katie slides on the sofa beside me and takes a deep breath.

"Katie, what am I going to do?" I hate how whiney I sound. I hate how small and thin my voice is, and how painful it is to say those words. Katie turns toward me and puts her hand on my forearm.

"You're going to breathe. Right now you're just going to breathe. Then you're going to go to work. You'll do your job, and you're going to be there for your daughter. *Do not* for a second think that you're going to run away from this. You've seen how Audrey has brightened since she moved here. You told me she was being bullied back in Seattle, and even after the accident she seems happy here. Plus, you said yourself that this job is a huge step for you."

"Yeah, but..."

Katie shakes her head. "The Clarkes are sexy, irresistible men," she starts. She looks at me and grins. "Trust me, I know. I'm a little jealous that Ethan is so in love with you."

"He's not–"

"Please, Zoe," Katie grins. She shakes her head. "He's in love with you. But all three of them have a wildness to them that no one can tame."

"He's an *arsonist*."

"He did what he thought was right. Most people here agreed with him, for what it's worth."

My heart shears again and I shake my head. "I can't approve of something like that. He *lied* to me about it."

Katie is quiet for a while. She pats my arm and takes a deep breath.

"Yeah," she finally says. "He did."

I look at my friend and the pain in my chest is almost unbearable. I finally felt like I'd found a place for my daughter and me to be happy. I'd moved up in my career. I'd found a man that I cared about. I thought he cared about me. But do I even know him? He committed a felony, and most importantly, he *lied* to me. *To my face!* I asked him a direct question and he didn't even have the guts to be honest.

"I'm just not sure if I can get over that," I finally say.

Katie takes a deep breath and nods. "That's understandable."

I brush hot tears off my cheeks and shake my head. My thoughts are muddled and I feel like a failure and a fool. I feel like a bad mother and an even worse daughter. I thought my life was going to get better by moving here, but it's only gotten worse.

"What do you want to do?" Katie asks. I look at her and see real concern in her eyes. I see friendship in them, too. I haven't had a real friend in so many years that the look in her eyes shocks me.

I open my mouth to answer when a blood-curdling scream floats down the hallway where my daughter disappeared. Both of us jump at the sound. I scramble to my feet.

My heart stops as my blood runs cold. I can only say one thing in a breathless, panicked whisper:

"Audrey."

34

ETHAN

Zoe isn't answering her phone, and my heart feels like it's dropped to my stomach. The anger that consumed me when I saw Margaret McCoy at the festival has disappeared. In its place is a dark hole in the center of my chest. I just need to explain to her how I feel about her.

My hands are shaking as I dial Zoe's number again. Dominic's heavy hand drops on my shoulder and I take a deep breath.

"She'll come around," he grunts. I turn to look at him and see real concern in his eyes.

I shake my head. "I don't know if she will."

Dominic says nothing, and the two of us wander out of the fair grounds. I glance down the street toward my house, and I wonder if Zoe went there.

Maybe she's getting all her things, packing them up to leave. The thought sends a sharp pain straight through my heart, and I squeeze my eyes shut.

"I fucked up," I say, looking at my brother. Dominic's eyebrows draw together, but he says nothing. He takes a deep breath and looks down the road with me. "I should have just told her the truth when she asked about the fire."

"You couldn't," Dominic says gently.

I sigh. I'm not sure how long we stand there. Dominic seems to understand that I don't want to say anything, but I appreciate his presence. Before long, Aiden's truck pulls up in front of us. His face is dark as he looks at us, killing the engine and sliding out to meet us.

"I heard what happened in there," he says, glancing behind us at the festival. I follow his gaze and scowl. Hearing the laughter and chatter and fair music is like a slap in the face. "What did Margaret say?"

"I don't even know anymore," I reply, suddenly exhausted. "I just snapped. I just got sick of pretending like I don't have this hatred for her inside me. Or like I didn't *enjoy* burning down that fucking hotel."

My brothers are quiet for a few moments, until Dominic clears his throat. "You guys want to get a beer?"

Harold's Bar is just a few doors down, so I shrug. "Sure."

The three of us walk in silence, with me flanked on either side by my brothers. Once again, I'm grateful that they're not talkative. I'm not even sure what I would say. The way I feel right now is hard to describe. It's like I have this searing pain in my chest, but at the same time the rest of me feels numb. When we sit down at the bar and I grab the beer that Harry puts in front of me, I can hardly feel the cool glass in my hand. My fingers are tingling slightly, but apart from that I feel nothing.

"She was the best thing that ever happened to me," I say when I've drank half my beer.

My brothers don't respond, and I take it as agreement. She was the best thing I ever had, and now I've lost her. Her, and Bernie, and Audrey. All three of them are beyond my reach.

I lift my beer to my lips as my phone starts buzzing. Just when I reach into my pocket to grab it, Dominic's phone starts ringing as well.

"Zoe," I say, just as Dominic says "Mara." We look at each other, and then at Aiden before answering the phones.

"Zoe," I answer, breathless. My heart is beating furiously against my ribcage, when a minute ago my chest was hollow.

"She's gone," Zoe's panicked voice answers. "Where is she!"

"Who's gone? Slow down, babe, come on," I say, my heart racing as I try to keep my voice calm.

"Audrey! I came to the hotel. I sent her to go find Mara and now she's gone and the baby's gone too!"

I can hear Mara's panicked voice behind her and I glance at Dominic. The blood has drained from his face and my heart starts thumping.

"I'll find her," I answer. "I'm sending Aiden to get you."

"Where did they go?"

"I don't know," I say. "But I'll find her."

I hang up the phone and all three of us stand up at the same time. Aiden tosses some money on the bar and stalks toward the door.

"Audrey and Hailey are gone," I explain as we go outside. Dominic is seething beside me, his face completely white and his hands balled into fists. I look at Aiden. "They're at the hotel. Go get Mara and Zoe. Dom, you go check your house and my house. Maybe Audrey took Hailey for a walk, or something. I'm going to head toward the airport."

Both brothers stare at me. "Airport?" Aiden says with a raised eyebrow.

My face darkens.

"You think Margaret McCoy has something to do with this? Skipped town with the kids?" Dominic growls.

"I don't know, but you know Margaret's history of disappearing. You saw her face back there."

Dominic nods and starts jogging toward his truck, parked down the street near the festival. I follow him and head toward mine. I nod to Aiden. "Call me when you're with Zoe and Mara, and go check the community center and the rest of the hotel."

Aiden nods without a word, and jogs toward his truck. I jump in the driver's seat of my vehicle and start the engine, gripping the steering wheel with both hands and trying to ignore the thumping of my heart.

My blood runs cold with fear as I rush down Main Street toward the freeway. I press the pedal down a little bit further as my mouth goes dry. I need to keep my hands on the steering wheel to keep them from shaking. My phone rings, and I put Dominic on speaker.

"Not at my house," he says. "I'll check yours. Any luck?"

"Not yet," I say with a strained voice. "Hold on, Aiden's calling." I hang up and answer Aiden's call. "Yeah?"

"They've checked the hotel from top to bottom. They're not here. The baby's diaper bag is still here and there's no sign of Audrey. It's like they just disappeared into thin air."

"Smells like Margaret," I say through clenched teeth. Aiden grunts in response as my heart hammers in my chest. My eyes narrow as I stare down the highway, trying to see a car in front of me. If I've gone the wrong way, I'm speeding in the opposite direction and I'll never find them.

My eyes widen at the thought. "Fuck," I say under my breath. If Margaret did take them, she'll be banking on me racing toward the airport. I'll get there in three hours and by that time she'll be long gone.

Following my instinct, I check my rear-view mirror and slow down to do a quick U-turn. Soon, my foot is pressing the pedal down and I'm racing back toward Lang Creek. My heart is in my throat and my vision is blurring along the edges. I lean forward until my chest is almost touching the steering wheel, and all I can do is take short, shallow breaths to keep myself from passing out.

I need to find them. Hailey is my niece, and Audrey is becoming like a daughter to me. My phone rings again and I see Zoe's number.

"Ethan," she says as I put her on speaker. The anguish in her voice pierced through my heart and I take a deep breath.

"I'll find them, Zoe," I say. "I promise."

"I'm sorry," she breathes. "I'm sorry."

"What are you sorry about? Stop it, Zoe." I struggle to say as a lump forms in my throat. "I love you and I love Audrey and I'm going to find them."

She sobs, and my fear turns to anger. I'll find them, and Margaret McCoy should pray for her life if she's the one who took them.

35

ZOE

I'M SHAKING. Panic is coursing through my veins like a drug, and I cling to the dull hope that Audrey is somewhere safe with Hailey.

"Maybe Audrey took Hailey out for a walk," Mara says, staring at me with the same blind look in her eyes. Her face is paler than I've ever seen it, and she's shaking just as hard as I am. "You know how she loves to spend time with the baby."

I try to swallow past the huge lump in my throat. I nod. "Maybe," I reply. "It wouldn't be like her to just take off like that though." The stroller was still there as well, but I don't mention that.

Mara says nothing. She stares out the window as Aiden drives us toward Ethan's house. The anger I felt only an hour ago has completely disappeared. Now, I want nothing more than to feel Ethan's arms around me and to have Audrey beside us. I've never felt happier than when I'm with both of them, and a lie that Ethan told to protect his brothers seems trivial now.

My heart is thumping as we drive up to the house. It's completely dark, exactly how we left it this morning. Both Mara and I fall out of the truck and stumble toward the house. My hands are shaking as I try the doorknob and find it locked, and then struggle to fit the shiny new key that Ethan just gave me into the old lock. When I finally open it, we rush inside, but I already know the girls aren't there.

Mara hangs onto my arm, her nails digging into me as she looks up at my face in anguish. She opens her mouth but nothing comes out, and I hear the soundless scream of her agony echoing with my own.

Aiden's face is dark as he checks the yard. He comes back around the front and shakes his head. His lips form a thin line.

"Walk me through it again. When was the last time you saw the girls?"

"I was putting Hailey down for a nap," Mara says impatiently. "I've already told you everything!"

"Go through it again."

"I put Hailey down for a nap in the nursery and went over to the office. It's just down the hall!" She says, clinging onto me. "I didn't hear a thing! Audrey came up to me then, with the sales figures from yesterday. She said Katie had given them to her."

"She did," I say. "Katie was with me."

"Then, Audrey left and I assumed she'd be with you. I finished my paperwork and went to check on Hailey, and…"

Aiden scowls. "Right. So either Audrey took Hailey somewhere, or somebody else took them both. They had to leave through the side door for neither of you guys to have seen them," he reasons. "Who has access to the side door? Is it locked?"

Mara nods and I can see her struggling to swallow. She puts her hand to her forehead and takes a long, shuddering breath.

"Who would take them?" Mara says. Her face is drawn, and the pain is written all over it. I put my arm around her to distract myself from the pain in my chest.

I take a deep breath. "We left the festival after the scene with Ethan and Margaret. She was staring at me with such hatred," I shiver, remembering the look the woman was giving me. "I was so focused on Ethan," I continue.

I look at Mara. "Do you think...?"

Mara's face crumples. "Do I think my own mother could have taken my daughter? Is that what you're asking me, Zoe?"

My heart breaks all over again and tears start falling from my eyes. "I'm sorry. I'm so sorry, Mara, I didn't mean it."

Mara laughs, but there's no humor in it. She shakes her head. "I'm upset because the answer is *yes*." She looks at me and her eyes are so full of pain that it's hard to hold her gaze. She shakes her head again and tears fall down her cheeks. "Yes, I think my mother took my daughter and yours, and I don't know where she's going or what she'll do. I thought if I let her get to know Hailey, that maybe... I don't know!" She says, staring up at the ceiling. She shakes her head. "Maybe we could fix this fucked up relationship. Maybe my mother could be a part of my life."

She's still holding onto my arm, and she squeezes it tighter. Fear grips my heart like a hand, squeezing the life out of me as Mara's words sink in. She thinks her own mother took her daughter, and mine too. I don't know if Audrey was just caught in the crossfire, or if Margaret has some malicious intent toward me, too.

"Right," Aiden says, and we both jump. His voice is deep and commanding. "We're going to operate on the assumption that Margaret has the girls. Where would she go?"

"I have no fucking idea," I respond, looking at Mara for an answer.

She shakes her head, and tears keep falling down her cheeks. "I realized when she left last time that I know nothing about her. I don't even know who my mother is."

I wrap my arms around Mara and squeeze her close, then pull away and put my hands on her arms.

"Mara, you're the strongest woman I've met in a long time. You gave birth to your daughter in your own house without a complaint, and we are not going to let that woman take our girls away from us."

Mara nods, and I look at Aiden. "Where do we look?"

"Well, Ethan has gone in the direction of the airport. He'll try to overtake her, but it's unlikely that she'll be taking the highway, so he might have to drive to the airport and wait it out."

"The airport is hours away! What if she didn't go to the airport?" I ask, glancing at the wilderness that surrounds us. "She could be anywhere."

Aiden's face darkens and he grunts. Despair starts seeping into my bloodstream, and I fight to hold it off. This is all too much. From my mother's death, to finding out about Ethan and the fire, to now losing Audrey, I feel like every strand of love in my life is slowly, tortuously being unraveled. The pain is almost too much to bear.

Before I can spiral any further, Aiden's phone rings. He answers with a grunt, and then listens for a few moments.

"See you there," he says, and hangs up with another grunt.

"Who was it?" Mara says, going to him and putting her hands on his chest. She wraps his shirt in her fists and hangs on to him as if she's about to collapse. "Do they have Hailey?"

"Ethan," he says. "He's not going to the airport. He thinks Margaret has them too, and he thinks she's going to the river."

"The river?" Mara and I answer in unison.

Aiden says nothing. He turns and walks back to his truck. Mara and I have time to exchange a panicked glance before rushing to follow him. I taste blood in my mouth as I climb back into the car. My heart is racing and my shirt is sticking to the sweat on my back. I feel like I can't breathe any deeper than the shallowest of breaths, and I hold on to the car door with all my strength to keep myself from crumpling into a heap.

Aiden revs the truck and we fishtail as he speeds down the gravel road toward Lang Creek.

36

ETHAN

I MIGHT BE wrong about this. I could be taking Aiden, Mara, and Zoe away from wherever the girls are. I could be leading them on a wild goose chase.

I could be wrong, but I don't think I am. I saw the hatred in Margaret's face when I told her she was pure evil. I saw the fury in her eyes when I told her I'd burn down her hotel a thousand times over. I *know* that she came back for revenge, and it would be just like her to cut us all where it hurts the most: our kids.

Her look told me enough—I just had to realize what she was saying. She wants my brothers and me to feel pain. She always has. Ever since my father, her lover, died, she's blamed the three of us brothers for his death. She's blamed her daughter for it, too. It was Mara my dad jumped in the river to save.

His death hit us all differently, and at the Fall Festival, I saw the depth of her pain. Instead of dealing with it, she's let it fester for a decade, until the original wound is almost unrecognizable. She's turned into a vindictive, bitter person. She's tried to take business and love away from the three of us brothers. It hasn't worked.

Until now.

Now, with Audrey and Hailey in her custody, she can bring ruin to both Dominic and me. She can see how much he cares for his daughter, and how much I care for Zoe and Audrey. She sniffs love out like a bloodhound, and now she's trying to end it.

I know it in my soul. I know that she has them, and in her mind, it's the final payback for my father's death.

I haven't been back to that spot by the river since my father died. It's on the opposite end of town to where Audrey fell in. There, the river bends and there are many rapids and eddies and undercurrents that make the already frigid water turn lethal.

If I were a crazed, bitter woman intent on hurting two little girls in some sort of twisted poetic justice, I'd bring them there.

My heart is in my throat as I turn off the main road onto the gravel path that leads toward the river. The trees are thick here, blocking out most of the light from the sun. It's been dry, so the truck bounces along the gravel road kicking up a big cloud of dust behind me.

I tighten my hold on the steering wheel and push my foot further down onto the pedal. Images of my childhood are flashing through my mind. My brothers and I used to walk down this path with my parents, hauling picnic baskets and fishing poles to spend the day by the river. We'd run ahead, laughing and playing, throwing sticks and rocks into the river once we got there.

I haven't been back since my father's death, but it all looks the same.

The trees are sparser when I get closer to the river. I see Margaret's car parked on the side of the road and my heart jumps in my throat.

I wasn't wrong, and somehow that makes me feel even worse. My worst nightmare is coming true. I know Aiden, Mara, and Zoe aren't far behind, but there's no time to wait. I start running toward the little path through the trees that leads to the clearing where my father jumped in to save Mara over a decade ago.

Hesitating, I glance back at my truck and rush back. I grab a length of rope and sling it over my shoulder, sprinting back toward the trees. If someone falls in the river, I'm going to need something to haul them back in. Or as a worst case, I'm going to need something to hold onto when I jump in to get them.

I can't hear any birds, or any rustling of leaves. The forest is deathly quiet as I run. My footsteps sound too loud, and I'm panting as I try to speed up. My foot slips and I almost roll my ankle on a tree root. I swear and jump to save myself at the last second. I hold out my arms and catch myself on a branch before continuing my sprint through the forest.

The rushing water is getting louder, and I try my hardest to hear something else. *Anything* else. Crying, or screaming, or voices. I need to know that they're still here. Still alive.

The trees thin and I can finally see a glimpse of the river. My heart starts pounding even harder as I see flashes of memories in my mind. They're all muddled together. I see happy memories, when both my parents were alive. Then, I hear Mara's panicked screams when she fell in as a teen. I can still see the look of terror on her face right before she went under. I remember the way my father ran in, the way the water splashed around him. I can still remember the fear in everyone's face and the relief when he brought her back. I remember the hospital, and the weeks of darkness that followed.

The memories pulse through my mind at a dizzying speed, one by one with every step I take closer to the water. Finally, the trees clear and my stomach lurches.

They're here.

They're alive.

Margaret has her back to me, and she's pushing the two girls out toward the worst of the rapids in an old, rickety tin canoe. She wades in, thigh-deep, and pushes the dilapidated watercraft out toward the rushing water.

That's when I scream. Audrey is holding Hailey in her arms, and just as Margaret's hands leave the boat, Audrey's smile melts away and her face is gripped with a terror so strong it makes my heart ache. She sees me then, and I think she screams my name, but I don't hear anything.

I just see Margaret, turning toward me and snarling. Audrey is looking back at the rushing white water behind her, and then turning back and yelling something toward me. She can't move with the baby in her arms.

Margaret rushes toward me in a low crouch. She looks as if she's part panther. At the same time, I drop the rope from my shoulder and get ready to fling it toward the girls as I run to the water's edge. Audrey is clinging on to the baby, and the boat is getting closer and closer to the rushing water. It's rocking from side to side. Even from the banks, with Margaret just about to crash into me, I can see the whites of Audrey's eyes when she looks at me in fear.

Margaret's wily body crashes into mine and we roll on the ground. She's like a wildcat. She bites and scratches and hangs onto me with all her might. I manage to throw her off and run toward the water.

"Audrey, catch this rope!" I scream as I hurl the rope toward her. I watch as the boat rocks when Audrey moves, holding the baby in one hand and trying to extend her other arm toward the rope. It lands across the front of the canoe and the boat rocks dangerously from side to side. It's just out of Audrey's grasp, but before I can see if she gets it, Margaret attacks me again. She yells and pushes me to the ground, mashing my face into the rocks at the water's edge. I look up through one eye to see Audrey grab the rope.

I throw Margaret off and take hold of the rope, pulling the girls toward me.

"Tie it off on someth–" I don't finish, because Margaret is tackling me to the ground again. This time, I fall face first into the water. Water fills my nose and mouth, and my hands scrape the rocky bottom of the river. I'm disoriented and for a moment, I lose my grip on the girls' lifeline.

She's holding my head underwater as I flail and try to fight her off, grab the rope, and come up for air at the same time.

My lungs are burning as she holds me down. I can't get any leverage as the water washes over me and I slide on the rocks. I'm reaching around me, splashing frantically when I feel the rough thread of the rope against my arm. I grab onto it and hold it as tight as I can as my lungs scream for oxygen.

This could be it for me. In this moment, with a crazed woman holding me down, I could drown right here where my father jumped in to save another young girl over a decade ago. I cling onto the rope as my arms turn to lead and I know I'm losing this fight. My lungs are on fire, and I know I only have a couple seconds before my world goes dark.

Somewhere, in the back of my mind, I instinctively understand why my father jumped in to save Mara all those years ago. The anger and resentment I had for him melts away. When I face my own death, I finally make peace with his.

If my face wasn't being held underwater by a deranged woman, I might laugh at the beautiful irony of it all.

37

ZOE

THE OLD WOMAN screams when my nails dig into her scalp. I drag her back as Mara grabs onto the rope and Aiden lifts Ethan up out of the water.

We're all screaming. I'm screaming as Margaret slices her nails across my cheek. I'm screaming when I see Ethan's limp body in Aiden's arms. I'm screaming as Mara tries to pull the boat with our girls in it back to shore.

Mara is screaming at Audrey wordlessly, crying as she sees Hailey unharmed. Audrey is screaming. Hailey is wailing in her arms.

Aiden is yelling, slapping Ethan across the face to try to wake him up before he looks over to me and his eyes widen.

Margaret is screaming, too. She's yelling like a deranged demon as I stumble backward and she lands on top of me. She turns, her hair wild and her eyes cloudy as she wraps her cold hands around my neck. I struggle with her, pushing my fingers into her nostrils and eyes as I try to push her off me.

My other hand is crawling around me, looking for a rock, or a stick, or anything I can use to get this woman off me.

This must be what everyone calls a survival instinct. There are no thoughts in my head. None of my movements are conscious, and I don't see anything except Margaret, and the excruciating hold she has on my throat. Margaret tightens her hands around my neck and a terrifying smile appears on her lips. As the edges of my vision go dark, and I feel the strength start to leave my body, my hand finally finds a palm-sized rock.

I use every ounce of power that I have left, arcing my arm around and bringing the rock down as hard as I can on Margaret McCoy's head.

It hits her head with a sickening crunch, and Margaret's deranged eyes go dull. She collapses on top of me, banging her head against mine as I groan. Her hold on my neck loosens, and I take a deep, ragged breath. Aiden appears in my field of vision, pushing the woman off me and putting his hands on my face.

"You okay?"

He's breathless. I roll onto my side and cough, holding my neck with one hand and clinging onto the rock with the other. I feel a hand on my shoulder and look up to see Audrey.

Tears fill my eyes and she wraps her arms around my neck. I wince as she hits the same spots that Margaret was hanging onto, but it doesn't matter. Physical pain is nothing compared to the anguish that I felt before.

It only takes a moment for me to inhale sharply and sit up, looking over toward the spot where Aiden dragged Ethan. Panic washes over me again as I remember the limp, lifeless body that Aiden lifted out of the water.

My shoulders relax as I see Ethan leaning on his elbow, coughing and wheezing as he recovers. His lips aren't a sickening shade of blue anymore, and his skin isn't a deathly shade of white.

Mara is holding Hailey, silently crying and rocking her wailing baby to calm her down. Ethan looks up at me, and his eyes are filled with a million things we haven't said to each other. I wrap my arms around Audrey, holding her to my chest as Ethan and I look at each other.

Finally, I glance over at Margaret McCoy. She's still limp. Her eyes are closed and there's an ugly gash on the side of her head. Aiden is crouched over her, feeling her neck with two fingers.

My breath catches in my throat as Aiden looks at me with dark eyes.

"Did I..." I say, not wanting to finish my sentence. *Did I kill her?*

Aiden shakes his head. "I feel a pulse. Pass me that rope," he says to no one in particular. Ethan drags himself up and tosses the waterlogged rope over to his brother. He takes a few halting steps toward me and collapses next to me, wrapping his soaking wet arms around me. I melt into him, and he holds both Audrey and me in his arms.

"I'm sorry," he says as he leans his face into my neck. His voice is muffled when he says it again. "I'm so sorry."

I shake my head and reach back to stroke his hair. "Ethan, stop. You saved our girls. You were so brave. You figured out where they were. You," my voice catches. "You almost died."

Audrey takes a long, shuddering breath when I say the last word. She peels herself away from me and throws her arms around Ethan's neck. He falls backward, and she kisses his cheek.

"Don't die, Ethan," she says. "I like having you around."

A smile appears on Ethan's lips and my heart thumps in my chest. Ethan glances at me and his smile widens.

"Do you?" He asks, and Audrey nods.

"I don't like it when you and Mom fight."

"Me neither," he says as he ruffles her hair. "I hope we don't fight like that ever again."

I lay back onto his chest, and Audrey snuggles beside him. He wraps his arms around both of us and lets out a long sigh. "My girls," he says. He kisses the top of my head.

"You okay?" he asks.

"Yeah," I reply, even though I'm not quite sure if that's true. "I think she chipped one of my teeth when she collapsed on top of me though." I thumb the sharp edge of my tooth before lifting myself up and smiling at him. "See?"

He chuckles. "Chipped tooth or not, you're the most beautiful woman I've ever seen. And a fucking badass, too."

Audrey gasps. "Mom, he said 'badass'!"

I laugh. "I think he's allowed to say that right now. Just once, though."

Audrey looks at me, wide-eyed, and then glances at Mara with her mouth hanging open. Mara laughs and then kisses Hailey's forehead.

All five of us turn when we hear a crashing sound in the forest. Dominic comes barreling through the trees, his hair disheveled and his eyes wide as he takes in the scene in front of us. His eyes go straight to Mara and the baby and I see his face crumple as he starts to weep.

Mara goes to him, and the two of them cry together as they hold their infant. Aiden grunts, then, and I look over at him for the first time in a few minutes.

He's got Margaret tied up just as her eyes flutter open. She starts to say something, snarling as she looks at me, but he stuffs a bit of cloth in her mouth. He glances at Ethan.

"You might want a new sock," he says, pointing to the gag in the old woman's mouth. "Fell off in the struggle."

"I think I can manage that," Ethan says, squeezing his arms around Audrey and me again. "I guess we'd better get back to town and try to explain this mess."

"I called Bill," Dominic says. "He's on his way."

"Explain this mess is right," Sheriff Bill Whittaker says as he walks onto the gravelly strip of beach on the edge of the water. His boots crunch as he takes a few steps, hooking his thumbs into his belt loops and surveying the scene in front of him. "This'll take more explaining than the fire at that fucking hotel," he breathes.

"You managed that one okay," Ethan grins. "This should be easy."

"Fucking Clarkes," he mutters, shaking his head. He walks over and looks down at Margaret, who struggles against the ropes with fury in her eyes.

Bill grunts and shakes his head. "We'd better get that one to a hospital," he says, pointing his foot toward Margaret. "As much as I'd like to leave her here to rot, it wouldn't be ethical." He winks at me. "And I'm nothing if not ethical."

Aiden chuckles, and shakes his head. "Ethical is one word for it. I'm just glad your ethics seem to match mine most of the time."

"Bill," I squeak, looking at the sheriff.

He grunts at me, nodding.

"I don't want to go to jail."

That seems to surprise him, because he stands up taller and frowns. His thick eyebrows draw together like two caterpillars on his forehead. I glance at Margaret, and then hold up the rock that I'm still clutching in my hand.

"I did that."

Bill stares at the rock, and then at Margaret, seeming to take in the bloody gash on the side of her head for the first time. She's got red rivulets running down the sides of her head, covering her forehead and ear. She's stopped struggling, and her eyes are half-closed as her breathing becomes more labored.

The Sheriff takes it all in, and then he does something I don't expect. He starts laughing. He laughs so hard his hat falls off behind him. He clutches his belly and laughs until all of us are laughing with him. At first, we laugh tentatively, and then the stress dissolves into an almost manic laughing fit. Margaret doesn't react. I'm not quite sure why I'm laughing, but the emotion of the past couple hours releases in that moment.

Finally, Bill grunts as he leans over to pick up his hat. He brushes it off and places it back on his head, and then looks at me.

"Zoe Randall," he starts. "The only person going to prison is the woman who kidnapped your daughter." At those words, Margaret struggles against the ropes that Aiden bound her with. Bill and Aiden pick her up and drag her back toward the trees. I glance at Ethan, who smiles at me.

"You're one of us, now," he says with a grin. "Just a no-good criminal in a corrupt town."

His smile reaches all the way to his eyes, and I smile with him.

If this is a corrupt, criminal town, it's the nicest, most welcoming, most community-focused town of no-good criminals I've ever come across. I watch Bill and Aiden disappear toward their vehicles with Margaret, and I finally understand why Ethan started that fire. I understand him, because he's just like me. He just wanted to protect what was his.

I trail my fingers over his cheek and wrap them around the nape of his neck. Bringing my lips to his, I kiss him with a ferocity that I didn't know existed in me. I kiss him until I need to pull away just to catch my breath, and I lean my forehead against his. My heart beats for him and I smile.

"There's nowhere I'd rather be."

EPILOGUE
ZOE

"MOM!" Audrey yells, running through the front door. "Mom!"

I look over my shoulder at my daughter to see her beaming, brandishing a few pieces of paper in front of her.

"I did it!" She yells breathlessly, skidding to a stop in front of me. "I got 100% on my math test!"

I smile, wrapping my arms around her. "Congratulations, monkey. You worked so hard. You deserve it." I pull away from her and brush her hair off her forehead. She looks down at her test and flicks through the pages, smiling.

"Look, I even got the multiplication questions right, just like we practiced!"

She shows me her test and my heart grows. I ruffle her hair and give her another hug. "Good work, Audrey. Didn't I tell you that you could do it?"

She smiles at me and I see a glint in her eye. "Do you remember what else you said?"

I feign ignorance. "What did I say?"

"You said if I did well on this test, I could go with Ben and Rachael to go camping this weekend!"

I chuckle. "Did I say that?"

"Mom! I got *a hundred percent!* I can't do any better than that!"

"I'm joking, Audrey," I laugh. "Of course you can go. Ethan should be home any minute, he can help you get all the camping gear together. I called Ben's dad today to organize everything."

"Really?" Her eyes widen and she jumps from foot to foot. "I can go?"

"Of course, monkey," I say as Ethan walks in the door. That elicits a squeal from Audrey, who runs to him and wraps her arms around his waist. He looks at me, confused, and I just laugh.

THE NEXT DAY, when I wave goodbye to my daughter as her friends' parents drive her down our driveway, Ethan puts his arm around my shoulder and kisses my temple. I lean into him and inhale his scent, closing my eyes to enjoy the warmth of his body next to mine. He guides me back inside.

When we cross the threshold, Ethan closes the door behind us and turns toward me. He puts his hands on either side of my head, leaning against the closed door and caging me against it. A low growl rumbles through his chest and he presses himself closer to me, running his lips just above the skin on my neck.

"We haven't had the house to ourselves in a while," he says, and his voice sends a thrill through my body.

"No," I agree. "We haven't." I run my fingers up his shirt, feeling the warmth of his skin under my touch. He presses his chest against me, crushing his lips to mine and my whole body is set alight.

When his fingers crawl up my sides, I shiver. He presses me harder up against the door and a moan escapes my lips. I curl my fingers into his hair. Ethan grabs me by the waist and lifts me up so that I wrap my legs around him. He holds me close, carrying me toward the bedroom.

"You're the sexiest woman I've ever known," he says, his eyes betraying the fire of desire that's burning inside him.

"Almost as sexy as you," I say, grinding my hips against him as he groans. He throws me down on the bed and climbs on top of me, kissing every inch of skin that his lips come in contact with. I help him lift my shirt overhead and sigh as he runs his hands over my stomach. He kisses my clavicle and then moves down between my breasts and over my stomach, letting his lips brush over every bit of me.

I'm trembling. My desire is soaking my underwear and I claw at his shirt. He chuckles, helping me lift his shirt off so that I can see the hard planes of his body. My fingers trail over every ridge of his muscles and I bite my lip. Ethan looks at me with cloudy eyes, groaning as my hands explore his body for the millionth time.

When I unfasten his pants, his breath catches in his throat and he slides off me to take them off. Then, he undresses me slowly, tenderly, worshipping every inch of skin that reveals itself.

Every time he touches me feels like the first time. My skin is jumping under him, and my body is arching and quivering with every touch. He hooks his fingers into my panties, slowly peeling them down my legs as his eyes drink me in.

The way he's looking at me is driving me wild. He utters a deep, guttural groan when I kick my panties to the side and timidly spread my legs for him. I trail my fingers down my stomach toward my mound as he watches me, his eyes flashing with animalistic urges.

Then, he takes me. He plunges himself deep inside me and we become one. He wraps his arms around me and whispers everything and nothing in my ear. He sinks his teeth into my shoulder as I leave deep scratch marks on his back, and the two of us fly into the abyss together.

Some time later, Ethan lets out a sigh as I run my fingers up and down his arm. Our bodies are splayed on the bed with every movement slow and languid. He opens his eye and turns toward me, throwing his arm over my stomach and pulling me close.

"Marry me," he whispers in my ear. I pull my head back as my eyebrows arch upwards.

"What?"

"Come on, Zoe," he says, shifting so that we can see eye to eye. "We've built a life together here. Audrey is happy, I'm happy. I think you're happy," he grins. "I want you to be mine forever."

"Forever is a long time," I say, smiling.

"Not long enough," he responds, bringing his lips to mine. My fingers trace his jaw, wrapping around the back of his neck as I lean my forehead against his.

"Are you serious about this?"

"Completely."

My heart is thumping and my eyes are misting up. I try to swallow, but a lump has appeared in my throat. "And Audrey...?" I say, not quite sure exactly what I'm asking.

"I love her like a daughter, Zoe, you know that. You two are my family."

Tears are falling from my eyes and I laugh-snort as I curl my fingers into his hair. I lean my forehead against Ethan's and lay a trembling kiss on his lips. When we pull apart, he grins at me.

"So is that a yes?"

"Of course it's a yes," I say, laugh-snorting some more as I try to brush the tears off my face. "I love you, Ethan."

"Not as much as I love you," he whispers, and then crushes his lips against mine. His arms pull me closer and I melt into his broad chest, crying and laughing and smiling and snorting all at once. He laughs with me, and we make love again, basking in the happiness that we've built together.

~

EXTENDED EPILOGUE

ZOE

We drive up the winding road towards the site of the burnt-out hotel. Both Ethan and I are quiet, and I watch the dark, shadowy forest pass us by. The sky is clear, so I can see a thousand twinkling stars above us.

When the trees start to thin, Ethan slows down. My breath catches in my throat when the husk of the destroyed building comes into view. I haven't been out here in months. Ethan parks the car and stops the engine, taking a deep breath as we both look out over the site.

It's been about a year since I've been in Lang Creek, and the forest has definitely reclaimed most of the land. There are saplings growing up through the middle of the dilapidated hotel's lobby, and moss and ferns poking through everywhere. The moonlight gives the entire place an eerie feeling.

"If I believed in ghosts, I'd be totally freaked out right now," I say, breaking the silence that hangs heavy between us.

Ethan chuckles. "Good thing you don't believe in ghosts, then, right?"

I throw him a glance and nod to my door. "Come on," I say. "Let's go."

We step out of the car and I come around to his side. I slide my fingers through his and we start walking towards the charred shell of the building. The only sounds around us are crickets and soft rustling of the trees. Our shoes crunching on the gravel sound almost deafening.

When we get to the edge of the building, Ethan points to an area about thirty feet away from us.

"That's where I was," he says.

"That's where you dropped the match?"

He nods without a word. I slip my hand out of his and wander over to the area. I kick the gravel and take a deep breath, trying to imagine what it must have felt like to be in his shoes. Was he scared when he lit the match? Scared of being caught, scared of doing the wrong thing, scared of starting a forest fire?

Or maybe he wasn't scared at all. I glance over at Ethan, who's head is tilted towards the sky. His eyes are closed and he's breathing deeply. I smile. He doesn't look scared right now.

Our silence is interrupted by the sound of an engine. We both turn towards the road as I inch towards him. Before long, Aiden's truck parks up beside ours with Dominic not too far behind. Both brothers and their wives jump out of the vehicles and slam the doors with four quick, successive thuds.

"Hey," Aiden says to Ethan, extending his hand. Mara reaches me first, wrapping her arms around me. The six of us fall into a comfortable silence as we look out over the destroyed construction site that's slowly being taken over by the encroaching forest.

"I haven't been out here since the night of the fire," Dominic says to no one in particular.

"Well," I say, turning towards my new family. "I was thinking the other day that this fire, in one way or another, is the thing that brought us all together."

Maddy, Aiden's wife, tilts her head to the side and glances at Aiden. Mara smiles, and Dominic grunts. Ethan slides his hand over my shoulder and squeezes me close to him.

"So," I say, reaching into the bag that I've slung across my shoulder. "I brought marshmallows!"

They all exchange glances and I laugh, continuing. "What better way to celebrate the two year anniversary of this place burning down than to have a little campfire of our own!"

Dominic is the first to laugh. He takes two long steps towards me and wraps me in a big bear hug, lifting me off the ground and spinning me in a big circle. I laugh, holding onto him until he drops me back down.

"Well," Aiden says, his eyes gleaming in the moonlight. "What are we waiting for?"

The six of us trudge to the center of the site. We find a relatively clear space with some big cinderblocks that we can use as seats. We brush the moss and leaves away from a space for a campfire, and the brothers head off to find some wood while Mara, Maddy and I start arranging stones in a circle for a makeshift fire pit.

Mara looks at me and grins. "I didn't know you were so sentimental about this place," she says, sliding a cinderblock closer to sit on.

I laugh. "Neither did I. I was at work yesterday and someone mentioned the fire. Then I thought about you and Dominic, and you, Maddy, and Aiden. This fire is what made us family!"

"I never thought it would be a good thing, but it turned out to be the best thing that ever happened to me," Maddy muses.

"Same here," Mara says.

I laugh and shake my head. "Me too."

Ethan reappears from the darkness with an armload of wood. He drops it on the ground, crouching beside our little fire pit to start splitting it with a little hatchet he must have retrieved from his truck. Aiden and Dominic aren't far behind, and before long the three of them have their heads together as they try to get the fire started.

It only takes a couple minutes for us to have a happy little fire crackling in the center of our circle. We sit in couples, leaning against each other and staring at the dancing flames in silence. Aiden gets up and walks away, reappearing a minute later with a small flask.

"If the fire doesn't keep us warm, this might do the trick," he says in a gravelly voice. He hands me the flask and nods. "You do the honors," he says. "You're the one who brought us here tonight."

I nod to him and take a quick sip, grimacing as the liquid fire burns my throat. I cough and splutter as the five of them laugh at me. Handing the flask back to Aiden, I shake my head.

"It's stronger than I expected," I laugh. "You guys making moonshine now?"

He grins, sitting down beside Maddy and passing the flask to her. "No, but that's not a bad idea."

The six of us fall into an easy conversation. Then, Ethan tenses beside me and puts his hand on my knee. "Wait," he breathes, standing up. Everyone falls silent as he cranes his neck towards our cars.

I can hear it now, too. It's the unmistakable sound of an engine in the distance. He glances at me, frowning.

"You tell anyone else we were up here?"

I shake my head, swallowing hard. Ethan frowns and takes a step towards the road. "Stay here," he says to me. Aiden and Dominic get up with him, creeping slowly towards the entrance of the building site.

I look at Mara. "Who could it be? Should we be worried?"

Mara shakes her head, but her eyes are wide. "It should be fine. It's probably just some teenagers that had the same idea as us."

I nod, but my heart thumps as I watch Ethan and his brothers move towards the road as the sound of the engine gets louder.

ETHAN

My brothers and I creep towards the road, glancing at each other and motioning with hand signals. We shouldn't be here. It could be considered trespassing. We definitely shouldn't be starting a fire all over again. I'm a Ranger, for crying out loud. I *know* there's a fire ban on right now and I know the consequences. Still, I don't know anyone who comes up here anymore.

The car engine gets closer, and the three of us fan out to get better visibility on the newcomer. I glance over my shoulder at the campfire behind me, my heart squeezing in my chest as I think of Zoe.

If I get in trouble, that's fine. But her? She's got a prestigious job and a daughter to take care of.

I shake my head. I shouldn't be thinking like that. What's the worst that could happen? It's probably one of my coworkers doing their rounds. They'd probably laugh at the irony of our little campfire.

The vehicle sounds like it's getting closer. I can't see my brothers at all in the darkness of the forest, and my breath is getting shallower by the second. As the incoming car rounds the last bend, my heart starts thumping in my chest.

The nose of the car comes into view and I squint at the brightness of the headlights. I crouch down, shielding my eyes and trying to make out who it could be. My heart beats even faster when the car stops right there, with its headlights shining towards me. It doesn't park up next to our cars.

With the engine still running, I hear the car door open and heavy boots crunch on the gravel. Slow, deliberate footsteps sound as the person comes towards the front of the car.

"Well, well, well," comes a voice, just as the large body of Sheriff Whittaker is silhouetted by his headlights. "Looks like we've got some no-good criminals trespassing over here. Again."

I stand up straighter and chuckle, shaking my head as my brothers appear from the shadows. Bill laughs, hooking his thumbs into his belt loops. He leans back, shaking his head.

"Should have known it would be the Clarkes."

"We're just having a little celebratory bonfire," Dominic replies as he steps into the light that the car is emitting. "Seemed like as good a spot as any."

Bill laughs again. "You guys have a sick sense of humor."

"Care to join?"

"Fuck it," Bill says with a grin. "Why not."

He loops around to the driver's side door of his truck to turn off the engine, and then follows us back to our fire pit. The flames are roaring now, with a big, healthy fire keeping the girls warm. I take my spot next to Zoe, who looks at Bill and laughs.

"What are you doing here, Bill?"

He grins. "Well, I heard that all three of you guys had left your kids with Katie tonight and I knew you'd be up to no good. Is this your idea of a funny joke?"

Zoe laughs. "I guess it is."

"Well, I like it," Bill replies, setting his hat down beside him and spearing a marshmallow with a stick. "No better place to have a little campfire, if you ask me."

"That's what we thought, too," Aiden laughs.

We fall into easy conversation. We laugh about that night, two years ago, when Dominic, Bill and I stood out here and set the building ablaze. I shake my head, squeezing Zoe to my side.

Maybe she's right. It was what brought us all together. That hotel and the fire that destroyed it were what introduced all three of us to our partners and gave us new reasons to enjoy life.

Zoe toys with the ring on her left hand as it glints in the firelight. I grin.

"You still like your ring?" I ask. She extends her fingers, looking at the diamond on her finger and nudging her shoulder into mine.

"It's okay," she replies, glancing up at me and smiling. "Never thought I'd want to have another rock on my finger, but I'm starting to like having it there."

"You sure know how to flatter a guy," I laugh, and she winks.

"The last thing you need is flattery. Need to knock you down a peg or two."

"Why's that?"

A gentle smile floats over her lips and she runs the back of her fingers down my cheek. She tilts her chin up and lays a soft kiss on my lips before smiling at me again.

"Because you're too perfect and you know it," she finally says.

"That makes two of us," I reply, wrapping my arm around her shoulder as she nuzzles into me. We listen to the laughter and voices of my brothers, sisters-in-law and sheriff and fall into an easy silence. Zoe's hand rests on my thigh and I kiss the top of her head.

We stay like that until the fire dies down and then stand up to stretch and head towards our cars. When we get there, we all exchange hugs and goodbyes.

Mara wraps her arms around Zoe and squeezes her tight. "Thanks for bringing us up here," she says. "It was the perfect evening for it."

"I never thought I'd be celebrating arson, but it seemed appropriate," Zoe says, glancing at me as she smiles. We climb into my truck and I thread my fingers through hers as we drive back down the mountain towards the town of Lang Creek. Soon, we'll collect Audrey and go back to the cabin on the edge of the woods that we all call home. I glance at Zoe and squeeze her hand.

"You make me happy."

Her eyes shine and I watch her swallow as a smile lights her face. "So do you, Ethan. I feel like the luckiest girl alive."

"If this is how things work out, then I need to start burning down more buildings," I say, staring out the windscreen and trying to keep the smile from my face. Zoe laughs, smacking my shoulder and shaking her head.

"One is enough," she says, but based on the laughter dancing in her eyes, I know she'd be right there beside me dropping the match if she needed to.

We've come together in the most unlikely of circumstances. Against all odds, I've found my family, my wife, and my happiness.

~

SHOULDN'T WANT YOU

A SMALL TOWN ROMANCE

DESCRIPTION

My brother's best friend stole my first kiss, and then he left
town without saying goodbye.
Now, he's back...
...and I'm in trouble.

Love is a lie, and Sacha Black is the biggest fibber of them all.
Ten years ago, he told me he cared about me.
We kissed. I swooned.
He left.

Poof! Gone.
His kiss still echoing on my lips, his face still etched on my
brain.
G-O-N-E. Disappeared. Ghosted. Never to be heard from
again...

...until now.

My brother's getting married, and his best man happens to be
the one person I never want to see again.

Sacha Black is all grown up.
All man.
All muscle.
All thigh-clenching, cheek-burning, panty-melting *misery*.

The moment his stormy, gray eyes meet mine, I know my
poor heart doesn't stand a chance.

The only thing standing between us is ten years of pain and
my very protective brother.
Easy, right?

... Wrong.

1
———

WILLOW

THE BRIDE'S SHRILL, ear-splitting shriek pulls me from my conversation with the caterer. My head whips toward the noise as my heartbeat takes off at a gallop.

I've heard that noise before.

Not often, thankfully. I'm not *that* bad at my job—but I have heard it.

A funny thing happens when a woman gets married: her brain seems to fall right out of her head. It usually happens right about the time the dress shop nestles a veil in her hair. That thin, gauzy material has the power to transform the most reasonable woman into a monster.

Okay, okay. I know. I'm being unkind.

Not all women turn into bridezillas. Some of them are gorgeous and gracious and have perfect, fairytale weddings. More than one wedding has brought a tear to my eye and squeezed blood from the black rock in my chest.

Those aren't the women who turn my hair gray at the ripe old age of twenty-seven.

That high-pitched screech that just made all the glassware shudder?

That's not the sound of a fairytale wedding. That's the sound of something going very, very wrong.

"I have to go," I shout at the caterer, already taking off at full speed across the lawn. He says something I don't catch, because I'm already halfway back to the main hotel doors. I leave him to figure out how to stretch the two hundred meals into two hundred and fifty, because we learned this morning that the groom invited more guests at the last minute without telling us.

You know, standard stuff. Typical wedding planner problems.

My steps are silent on the grass as I run toward the back of the hotel. Employees are putting the finishing touches on the garlands of flowers and gauze that cover every available surface, and my vision zeroes in on the doorway.

Another scream reaches my ears, and I know I only have a few precious minutes to avert whatever disaster is happening upstairs.

I need to get to the bride.

When I first started as a wedding planner, I'd dress up for the events. I'd wear dresses and heels, thinking I needed to look fancy. My clothes were black, as always—I could blend in with the staff that way—but I chose formal, dressy outfits.

The problem with dressing up? You can't sprint in heels.

Now, I wear sensible clothing. Sleek black trousers with a lot of stretch in them paired with a smart top. Hair in a low bun. No jewelry.

Nothing too flashy. Nothing too remarkable.

Oh—and comfortable shoes.

Bursting through the hotel's doors, I take the stairs two at a time toward the floor reserved for the wedding party. A loud crash followed by more shouting lets me know things haven't calmed down.

I might be too late.

When I stop outside the bride's door, my chest is heaving. I can make out a few words amidst the shouting on the other side of the door, but I still can't figure out what's going on.

I don't know why I knock, but I do.

"Bethany?" I call out through the closed door.

Another crash rattles the door. I inhale, squeezing my eyes shut to steel myself against what's about to happen. I know what I'm in for.

More screaming. Probably tears. Some finger pointing and runny mascara.

My grip on the doorknob tightens as I suck a breath in through my teeth. My heart is still racing, and I pat my hair down to give myself some semblance of professionalism.

They'll probably blame me. They always do.

It's fine, I tell myself. That's what I'm here for. I do all the hard work for no recognition, and I take all the blame when things go wrong.

That's why they pay me exorbitant amounts of money to plan their weddings. That's why I was able to purchase my own house when I was twenty-two, and why I left college with no student debt. I've been able to build my own business from the ground up, without anyone else's help.

Not even the Black family, who owns half this town and used to own my family, too.

Still, getting screamed at can be tough.

With one last inhale, I push the door open, and all the breath is sucked out of my lungs.

Every time I think I've seen it all, something new happens. I've seen five-tiered cakes smashed to the ground. I've seen grooms walk out before the 'I dos' and brides throwing plates against walls. I've seen tears, breakups, fires, and car crashes.

Yes, literally.

I've never seen a woman staring in the mirror, holding frayed ends of bright, green, ear-length hair. I could have sworn that an hour ago, her hair was nearly down to her waist and blond.

"Beth—"

The bride's haunted eyes meet mine as her fingers comb through the damaged ends. A woman sits huddled in the corner, rocking back and forth in a bridesmaid's dressing gown. Her back is to me, and I read the words 'Bride Tribe' embroidered in gold thread across her shoulder blades.

The bridesmaid in the corner turns her head and I see her tear-streaked face. Her lower lip trembles. "I'm sorry, Bethany, I—"

"Don't." The bride's lips pinch, and the skin around her eyes tightens. She doesn't look at the woman in the corner. No one else moves.

The tension in the room tastes acrid on my tongue. Bethany drags her eyes back to the mirror as a shudder of revulsion courses through her body.

"Leave," she says in a flat, emotionless voice.

No one has to ask who she's talking to. The woman in the corner picks herself up off the floor, wringing her hands in front of her stomach. There's a splotch of white on her dressing gown—from bleach, maybe?

She takes a step toward the bride, opening her mouth to say something. She pauses, reconsiders, and then shuffles out of the room without uttering another word.

Bethany slumps down further into her chair, dropping her head in her hands. Her silky robe is pulled tight around her body and I can see tension and heartbreak rippling through her.

Guilt worms its way into my heart. I ran over here, thinking I'd have to appease a bride who had drunk too much champagne on an empty stomach and decided she wanted to replace all the white flowers with pink ones. I didn't think she would have burned all her hair off the morning of her wedding.

"I just wanted fresh toner put through my hair," Bethany says to no one in particular. "Christina just finished beauty school and she said she could brighten it for me. I didn't think she meant lightening it with bleach."

Tears cling to Bethany's eyelashes until she blinks them down her face.

She's not wearing mascara yet, thankfully. That's one less mess I have to deal with.

Producing tissues from my cross-body bag, I hand them over to her and put my hands on her forearms.

"We'll figure this out." My voice sounds more certain than I feel. I squeeze her wrists. "Okay?"

"I can't walk down the aisle looking like this," she whispers, tears now coursing down her face and dripping off her chin. "We have to cancel the wedding."

"If you cancel your wedding, you lose all your deposits, Beth," her mother chimes from the corner. "It's not that bad." She visibly winces as the lie slips through her lips. "You'll look back at this and laugh."

"Mom, I am *not* getting married with green hair. I can't even get extensions put in this mess."

Her fingers comb through the neon hair as her eyes move back to the mirror. Bethany's breath shakes as she stares at her reflection, and my cold, dead heart stirs.

I need to fix this. Not just because it's my job, but because this bride doesn't deserve to have her wedding ruined. She's one of the good ones. I thought today was going to be a fairy tale.

"What about a wig?" I ask, tilting my head.

The bride frowns. "A wig?"

"Let me make a phone call." I push myself up to my feet, plastering a smile on my face. Bethany stares at me, hope flaming to life in her eyes.

Another thing I've learned? If I exude confidence and calm, the bride can feel it, too.

"I don't want to look like I got my hair at Party City," Bethany whispers. "I'll be looking at these pictures for the rest of my life."

"You won't even be able to tell it's not your hair."

Smile. Confidence. Calm.

Bethany's lip trembles as she inhales, and she finally nods.

I glance around the room. There must have been some throwing of glassware and cushions, because it looks like a tornado hit the hotel.

I smile wider. "I'll get someone in here to clean this up. You need more champagne? I'll call the makeup artist to get started early."

Everyone in the room straightens up a bit, and the maid of honor puts her hand on Bethany's shoulder. The bride pats her friend's hand, and I back out of the room with measured steps.

Smiling. Confident. Calm.

As soon as the door closes, I'm scrambling for my phone.

"Jackson, I need you," I breathe as soon as my friend answers the phone.

"Girl, it's the asscrack of dawn and you're calling me on a Saturday morning. You know I work Friday nights."

"It's nine o'clock. Hardly the asscrack of dawn," I quip. "Please, Jackson. It's an emergency. A bride just bleached her hair off and she needs a wig. You're the only person I know who can install a lace-front with your eyes closed."

"Get a hairdresser! I'm off-duty. Miss Jackie needs her beauty sleep."

Jackson is not a morning person, especially not the morning after his weekly drag show.

But he has encyclopedic knowledge of wigs, and I don't know anyone else who can make this bride look like herself again.

I know I'm asking a lot, but I need him. Desperately. This is my livelihood. My business. Everything I've worked toward. It's the reason I can make my mortgage payments every month. It's the reason I don't need to ask the Black family for any handouts like my parents did.

I *need* this.

I let out a sigh, pinching the bridge of my nose. "I need Miss Jackie, Jackson. I need your magic."

A groan sounds over the phone, but I hear movement. A bed creaking. Rustling. My friend is getting out of bed and coming to my rescue.

"There better be an open bar at this thing," he groans. "You owe me one."

I grin, hopping from one foot to the other. "Thank you. Thank you. Thank you! I'll send you the address."

. . .

Not only does Jackson fit a gorgeous wig to Bethany's head, he makes her laugh and blush and feel beautiful again. Once he's done, you can't even tell that the hair isn't hers.

Bethany throws her arms around Jackson, who gives her two air kisses. The bride insists that Jackson stays for the reception, and I squeeze my eyes shut at the thought of telling the caterer that we need another meal. Jackson smiles and sways his hips out of the room. I follow after him, letting out a sigh of relief.

My friend glances over his shoulder. "You owe me one, Willow."

"I know."

"If I wasn't in dire need of some water and an Advil, I'd be telling you off for dragging me here to save your ass."

I fight a grin. "I think you like being the hero."

"There's nothing heroic about me," he replies, waving a hand. I see a hint of a smile on his lips, though, and the two of us walk side by side toward the area of the hotel set up for the wedding.

Jackson turns to look at me, tilting his head. "For someone who hates commitment and makes fun of weddings every chance you get, you sure did choose a funny kind of career."

"There's money in weddings." I shrug. "And I don't hate commitment."

A fine, groomed eyebrow arches as Jackson's dark brown eyes sparkle. His full lips purse and he shakes his head. "You know you're afraid of feeling anything. Ever since that boy left you high and dry, you haven't been the same."

Jackson turns around again, walking down the hall.

I scamper after him, protesting. "What boy? I don't know what you're talking about."

"You know *exactly* what I'm talking about." He shoots me a withering glance. "Or *who* I'm talking about, rather."

A lump lodges itself in my throat. He's right. Of course he's right.

I know exactly who Jackson is referring to, and it's a boy I've buried deep in my cold, dead heart. A boy I grew up with. A boy I thought I loved.

A boy who left without a word the day after he became my first kiss.

My brother's best friend meant the world to me and taught me exactly what I can expect from men: absolutely nothing.

No matter how gorgeous these weddings are, how much men will sweet-talk you, what they say means *nothing*.

Especially Sacha Black's sweet, honeyed words. They're the emptiest of the empty. The most meaningless, beautiful lies I'll never hear again. Hopefully.

"He's gone now, anyway," I say, speeding up to catch up with Jackson. "It doesn't matter."

I reach into my bag and pull out a sour lollipop, ripping the wrapper off almost savagely. I keep every bag, glove compartment, nook, and cranny stocked with these things. They help with the stress. As soon as the sweet, sour candy hits my tongue, I start to relax.

Jackson clicks his tongue. "You'll wreck your teeth with those things."

"Didn't know you moonlit as a dentist."

"I don't need to go to medical school to know that sucking on sugar eight hours a day is bad for your teeth. And stop avoiding the topic at hand."

"I thought the topic at hand was my oral health."

Jackson chuckles. "Oral fixation, maybe. Not enough of another type of lollipop in your life."

"Shut up," I say, a flush rising up my neck.

"If Young Mr. Black doesn't matter, why haven't you had a boyfriend in the past ten years, huh? Why are you pining after a boy who never thought about you twice?"

I wince at his words. A part of me still wishes Sacha cared about me. "I'm not pining after anyone."

"All you ever do is talk about how weddings are destined to fail, how you don't believe in true love, and how you don't think soul mates exist. Meanwhile, you have men throwing themselves at you every minute of the day and you pretend not to notice."

"No one is throwing themselves at me."

Jackson scoffs, shaking his head. "Yeah, right, girl. What about Benji?"

"The mechanic?"

"The *hot* mechanic who's been giving you puppy-dog eyes for the past six months. You know how I feel about a man bun. He's got that dirty, rough, working-man kind of sex appeal."

I shake my head. "He just fixed my car."

"He wants to do a lot more than fix your car, believe me."

"You're crazy."

"Uh-huh." Jackson flattens his lips. "You need to get over him. Sacha Black is *gone*. He's been gone for damn near a decade."

Even the sound of his name sends shivers tumbling through my veins. My breath catches, and Jackson doesn't miss a moment of it. The arch in his eyebrows tells me exactly what he thinks of my protests.

"Do you tell your clients you don't believe in love? You two-faced, lying little hussy?"

I fight a smile, shaking my head. "That would be bad for business."

"Mm-hmm." Jackson shakes his head. "I need a drink."

"This way." I grin, leading him to the bar. "Stay out of trouble. You may have saved the bride's hair, but we still need to make it through the rest of the day."

"Maybe you should start looking for trouble a little bit more, Willow," Jackson says as we walk up to the bar. "Might help you move on from a certain, gray-eyed beauty of a man."

A blush stains my cheeks, and all I can do is shake my head. "I have to go check on the caterer."

As I run away from my friend and all his truths, my heart stutters. I can't think of Sacha Black. I *can't*. He's the one man I allowed myself to care about, and the biggest mistake of my life.

I won't let that happen again—with him or anyone else.

Knocked Up by the CEO

Knocked Up by the Single Dad

Knocked Up...Again!

Knocked Up by the Billionaire's Son

The Complete Unexpected Series

Yours for Christmas

Bad Prince

Heartless Prince

Cruel Prince

Broken Prince

Wicked Prince

Wrong Prince

Lone Prince

Fake Engagement/ Fake Marriage Romance:

Engaged to Mr. Right

Engaged to Mr. Wrong

Engaged to Mr. Perfect

Mr Right: The Complete Fake Engagement Series

Mountain Man Romance:

Lie to Me

Swear to Me

Run to Me

The Complete Clarke Brothers Series

<u>Extra-Steamy Rock Star Romance:</u>

Garrett

Maddox

Carter

The Complete Rock Hard Series

<u>Sexy Doctors:</u>

Doctor O

Doctor D

Doctor L

The Complete Doctor's Orders Series

<u>Time Travel Romance:</u>

The Cause

<u>A little something different:</u>

Second Chance: A Rockstar Romance in North Korea